The Red Mask

Wendy Sheedy

PublishAmerica
Baltimore

© 2005 by Wendy Sheedy.

All rights reserved. No part of this book may be reproduced, stored in a retrieval system or transmitted in any form or by any means without the prior written permission of the publishers, except by a reviewer who may quote brief passages in a review to be printed in a newspaper, magazine or journal.

At the specific preference of the author, PublishAmerica allowed this work to remain exactly as the author intended, verbatim, without editorial input.

First printing

ISBN: 1-4137-8093-8
PUBLISHED BY PUBLISHAMERICA, LLLP
www.publishamerica.com
Baltimore

Printed in the United States of America

THIS STORY IS DEDICATED TO MY MOTHER. THANK YOU FOR HELPING ME TO TEACH MY CHILDREN TO PURSUE THEIR DREAMS. NOTHING IS MORE IMPORTANT.

~ **W.S.**

Chapter 1

It was one of those summer afternoons that one only dreams of. The sun was dancing upon the water of the bay causing the small rhythmic waves to sparkle as they reflected its light. A sailboat coasted by. The white jib sail and frothy white wake contrasted with the rich blueness of the water. The distant hill across the bay was dotted with brightly colored cottages that were surrounded by weather beaten Georgian Bay Pines and the waving emerald grasses of the season. The intense summer sun shone on the trees. An occasional fluffy white cloud would silently drift by, creating darkening patches that softly moved across the distant hillside.

The flawlessness of the August day was blurred for Courtney Myers. She sat on the clover-covered hillside, oblivious to the intense beauty of her familiar surroundings. Her arms were tightly wrapped around her tanned legs and tears were falling from her deep brown eyes. Rocking her petite frame back and forth in a fluid like motion, she hugged her legs even tighter in an attempt to stop the pain that was now intensifying in her stomach. Her despair was deepening, as she sat wondering why? Her fiancé, Brad Laduke, had unexpectedly ended the relationship. The wedding was still planned for later that month. Despite their long engagement, he had chosen now, of all times, to end things between the two of them.

The summer wind blew, carrying the sweet smell of the mint that also grew wild through the grass. Courtney wove her delicate fingers through her long hair that had blown gently across her face. Her native ancestral roots had blessed her with the shiny black mane. As the solitaire diamond of her engagement ring caught on a strand of her hair, she exclaimed "Damn!" as she attempted to unravel it. A young couple went by on a seadoo, laughing and obviously enjoying their day together on the water. Their laughter drove straight through to her heart. Staring at the diamond that reflected the summer sun, she remembered the wonderful times in her relationship with Brad.

They had formally met on a camping trip with mutual friends. The attraction between them had been instantaneous. Brad exuded pure masculinity and Courtney was immediately drawn to his rugged maleness. Although Courtney had known of Brad, she had never really known him other than a casual nod or an informal hello. They had wondered after they officially started dating, why they had never developed a relationship earlier in their lives? It was, after all, a typical small Ontario town where everybody practically knew everyone else.

Their commonalities seemed astonishing. They both possessed an adventurous fun-loving spirit and an overt desire to make a difference in the lives of others. The physical attraction between them was more than evident to their friends who bore witness to the immediate connection the two shared. The first night of the camping trip, Courtney had sat up until the wee hours with Brad, enjoying their time around the campfire. She quickly knew she wanted him in every sense of the word, but fought to hold on to her mounting desire. She had never given of herself to a man, as she deeply believed she should wait until she met the right man to share that gift. It was the third and final night of the trip, when Brad slipped into her tent. Her life was forever changed that night.

* * *

There had been little sign that the relationship was in trouble, other than Brad's initial reluctance to set a date for the actual ceremony. As she sat in her embryonic state, Courtney thought hard about the past two years. Rarely disagreeing on issues, it had seemed to be one of those blissful partnerships. They had agreed within months of meeting to become engaged. However, despite Courtney's attempts to set a date for the wedding, Brad had been somewhat elusive. It was last Christmas, a year after the engagement, that he had finally agreed to an August wedding the following summer. Although a little discouraged by Brad's lack of initial commitment,

Courtney justified his reluctance, assuming he was just being overly cautious about a very important life decision. She easily forgave his hesitation, once the date was finally set. Brad had apparently put aside any doubt he may have had.

When Brad had arrived at her door three nights earlier, he seemed extremely anxious. As he paced the apartment floor, Courtney assumed that something had happened at work to upset him. He explained to her that he loved her very much, but had felt that he just couldn't go through with the wedding. He said he felt unsure about the whole institution of marriage and was afraid that he had set the date because he was feeling pressure to do so. Despite Courtney's attempts to reason with him and tell him that what he was feeling was, quite naturally, last minute jitters, he remained firm that he had felt this way for months and that it wasn't just a case of 'jitters'. "Please Courtney," he had begged. "Don't try to change my mind on this. I will certainly weaken my stand, if you do. It hurts me to hurt you, but if I change my mind and marry you, I fear that I will regret my decision for the rest of my life."

Courtney had pleaded that maybe they should just postpone things until Brad felt surer about his commitment. Brad insisted that he felt that his feelings about marriage would not change. "I guess I'm just not the marrying kind, Honey." He had gently slipped his key to the apartment on the kitchen table. Courtney could feel the anger slowly build within, and his endearment had added salt to her wound. *Why would he wait so long to confront his reluctance to walk down the aisle?* The replies to the invitations had been returned months ago. The dresses, tuxedoes and flowers had been ordered. The church and reception hall had been booked and the menu had been selected. They had participated in two bridal showers hosted by each respective family and through all of the prenuptials; Brad had shown no sign of his true feelings. Her pleading with him did not alter his decision. As a matter of fact, it had only seemed to strengthen his resolve.

As Courtney wiped the warm tears away from her face, she was beginning to think about the monumental task of undoing all of the preparations she and others had worked so hard on. She realized that all of that was, of course, secondary to the loss she felt over her relationship with Brad, but it had added to the stress of the last three days. She had put off telling her family and friends about the current state of affairs, secretly hoping that Brad would call and tell her that he had made a terrible mistake. With each passing day, she was beginning to realize that Brad was truly firm in his decision. Despite her attempts to call him, he was not answering the phone or returning the many messages that she had left. His obvious avoidance of her hurt her even deeper. After all that they had shared, he wouldn't even talk to her. The past three days had been a living hell.

The tears continued to stream down her face biting hard at her skin. "Why? How could you do this Brad?" The wind carried away her words. As if expecting an answer from the seagulls that flew overhead, or the boats that drifted by, she was waiting for some divine answer to her question. As she closed her eyes, the sun created a red backdrop in her mind. Two black dots formed on the red canvass beneath her eyelids. For a second, she saw the image of a face and she opened her eyes in an attempt to readjust her vision.

Although this place had always been her place to come and meditate, she had often shared it with the man she planned to marry. Her sadness was increasing, just being there. Courtney slowly got to her feet knowing her quest for answers had not come to fruition. Discouraged and feeling even sicker in the depth of her stomach, she started towards the parking lot where she had parked her Neon. She turned one more time, half hoping to have some deep revelation into what had caused the demise of the relationship. None was forthcoming, so she continued up the hill away from 'her place' and 'their place'. She would simply have to turn the page on this place, as difficult as that would be. It would only hurt more to come back.

* * *

Driving away from the place of their once shared dreams, she tried to imagine the reaction from their family and friends. How would she explain the situation to others, when she didn't even understand it herself? She clenched the steering wheel tightly with her right hand. Courtney didn't believe that time would ever heal the wound that Brad had left her with. There was no answer to the way he had ended the relationship. All she had wanted was some sort of reason why? She had prayed for some sort of justification.

As she looked up at the curve in the road in front of her, she was shocked to see that she had drifted into the opposing lane. The car heading towards her caused a wave of tingly shock to travel through her body. Braking hard, her car slid to a sudden stop on the dirt shoulder of the road. Her head whipped back, hitting the small headrest attached to the driver-side seat.

The pain shot hard through her head. The light of the sun shone brightly through the windshield of her car, filling her mind with the image of the red face. Blinking, Courtney looked up in shock at the blurred image of the elderly man who was exiting the other car. He was walking away from the silver sedan and proceeding over to Courtney. Opening her car door, the man gently asked, "Are you okay ... uh, miss?" She nodded that she was, despite the now intense ache in the back of her head. "I'm ... I'm so terribly sorry," she stammered. "You should be more careful! Do you need an ambulance?" Courtney was insisting that she was okay. "I am so sorry," she whispered. She watched as the elderly man returned to his car. He was shaking his head in a negative gesture. Courtney thought that he was probably thinking what a stupid person she was. She hit the palm of her right hand hard against the steering wheel. "Damn it!" she exclaimed. The pain in the back of her head seemed to strangely balance the sick feeling in the pit of her stomach. She put her car into drive and continued on her way, attempting to focus on the road in front of her car. *'Please'*, she pleaded with her mind. *'Please, let me focus.'*

* * *

Courtney arrived back at her large one-bedroom apartment located above the town's drugstore. She was still shaken from the earlier incident and the dull ache in the back of her head had not diminished.

The store was situated in the heart of the town on the main street that ran to Midland Bay. It had been a fixture on the main street, as long as Courtney could remember. Much had changed in the town over the years. The baby boomers from the city were now reaching retirement age, and were picking Midland as a place to live because of its peaceful beauty and proximity to Georgian Bay. Trendy shops replaced many of the vacated stores of yesteryear, but the drugstore remained, a silent tribute to the town's past. Above the store on the outside of the building, was a large painted mural depicting an old time apothecary. In the old days, druggists were virtually chemists mixing their own cures for people's ailments. The mural was one of the many murals that turned the downtown into a beautiful outdoor art gallery.

Courtney's parents lived not far from her in one of the town's nicer older areas. Her father was one of the few town doctors, and her mother spent her time volunteering at the local hospital. Although her parents expressed their disappointment when Courtney had decided to move out on her own the year before, they secretly knew that Courtney needed her own space. As the relationship between her and Brad seemed secure, particularly after the wedding date had been set, they never discussed their initial disappointment further with Courtney. Although Brad still lived technically at his parents' house, he would usually spend his nights at the apartment. Courtney didn't understand why they just didn't admit they lived together. Brad had insisted that it just wouldn't look right. Given the current situation, she wondered now if it was all part of Brad's fear of commitment.

As she looked around at her sparsely decorated apartment, she couldn't help but remember all of the times that they had shared there. When Courtney and Brad had first viewed the apartment, there was actually a beer bottle stuck in the hallway ceiling. The bedroom had a pair of old high-top sneakers crazy-glued to its ceiling. She remembered laughing at the ridiculousness of the sight. The apartment had not been painted in years and the walls had yellowed with time. Brad had helped her plaster and paint the apartment to make it more livable. They had planned to live there after they were married, but only until they found an affordable house to make their own.

Brad worked as a police officer on the local Midland police force. He had been a cop for almost four years. His father was a retired police officer and was extremely proud that his son had followed in his footsteps.

Courtney had graduated from college with a diploma in Hospitality and Tourism and was seeking a position at one of the local tourist resorts in the Midland area. In the interim, she was working nights at a local bar. 'Charlie's' was located in a neighboring community called Penetanguishene. Locals and tourists combined to make the bar an interesting place to work. There was a symbiotic relationship between the two types of patrons. Although they didn't always like each other, they knew they needed each other. However, despite their differences, most of the customers liked Courtney for her warm, friendly personality. She was a beautiful girl, and she regularly tolerated the drunken passes of several of the male patrons, along with the looks of disapproval from their dates.

Courtney went to the kitchen and grabbed a garbage bag from under the kitchen sink. She started searching desperately through the apartment for signs of Brad. She rummaged through the medicine cabinet in the bathroom. She tossed Brad's toothbrush, shaving cream, razors, comb and cologne into the bag. The faint smell of the bottle of cologne caused a further knot to form in her stomach. She had once loved the masculine scent, but now it only sickened her. She went into the bedroom and pulled out several items of Brad's clothing that were hung neatly in the closet. She shoved the clothes into the bag, as well. She dumped the entire middle drawer from her dresser that housed his underwear, socks and t-shirts into the bag. She continued through the entire apartment and threw in anything that reminded her of him; hunting and boating magazines, books, photographs of the two of them together, CD's of the music they had once enjoyed. When she was finished scouring the apartment for signs of Brad, she hastily tied the top of the garbage bag and threw it into the back of her closet. Although it would bother her that it was there, she still didn't throw the bag out. She still harbored a hope, deep within, that he would have a change of heart, and tell her he had made a terrible mistake.

* * *

That evening was one Courtney's few nights off work and she knew that she would have to face the inevitable with her parents. She called the house and her father's authoritative voice rang through on the answering machine. "You have reached the home of Doctor and Mrs. Myers ... as we are unable to take your call at present ... please leave a number where you can be reached and we will call you back as soon as possible." Courtney waited for the seemingly countless beeps to end. She quickly exhaled and cleared her throat before leaving a message. "Mom ... Dad ... it's me. I'm not working tonight. I thought I'd come by ... say ... around seven. I'll eat before I come over. Any problem, call me back ... otherwise, I'll see you then ... Bye."

As Courtney hung up the phone, she could feel a lump of deep emotion well up in her throat. She could only imagine her parents' reaction to the news. Courtney thought of how her mother would hold her and say that Brad was a terribly selfish person. Her mother would be extremely empathetic. Her father's reaction would not be as predictable. Courtney imagined he would initially question how Brad could do such a thing, and then he would turn his focus on Courtney. Brad was everything Dr. Myers had hoped for in a son-in-law, and Brad's father and he had become very good friends. They had been casual friends for many years, long before Courtney and Brad had met. The friendship grew deeper with the engagement of their children. Courtney's father would probably look for some way to reconcile the situation. Deep inside, she hoped her father's intervention would help.

Courtney grabbed the now depleted photo albums off of her living room floor and put them back on the makeshift bookcase that Brad had made for her out of wood and bricks. She was dreading that evening and decided she needed to speak to someone else about what had happened. Picking up the phone, she dialed her best friend. "Pilot Financial, Jodie Jackson speaking." Courtney was relieved to hear her maid of honor's cheerful voice on the other end of the phone. "Hey Jode, it me." Jodie let out a squeal of delight. "Hey, how's the bride to be?" Jodie was her usual chipper self, and it made Courtney wish even more that things were not the way they were. "Well ... actually. I need a favor. What time are you off today?" Jodie seemed to be thinking. "Well, it's dead here. I could leave around four-thirty. You want to get together?" Courtney was relieved. "Yes. Could you meet me at the Boathouse?" The Boathouse was a waterfront restaurant with a huge outdoor patio that overlooked the Midland Marina. Although touristy because of its proximity to the town dock, it was close to Courtney's apartment and to Pilot Financial. "Okay, Courtney. I'll meet you on the patio at four-thirty."

* * *

Courtney had been waiting for Jodie for a while. Jodie was always notoriously late and Courtney's inner anxiety had forced her to be early. "Hey girlfriend!" Courtney smiled at the familiar greeting. "Hey yourself. I ordered you a beer." Jodie smiled. "Excellent. I need one!" Courtney exhaled softly. She hated the feeling that she was the one who had truly *needed* a drink. Courtney had lost her appetite three days earlier, but when the waitress returned with the beers, she hastily ordered a burger. She knew full well she would take a bite and that would probably be it.

"Hey, have you heard about the Indian burial ground?" Courtney looked blankly at her friend. "God, Courtney! It's all over town! They hit it this afternoon!"

Jodie proceeded to tell Courtney about how some backhoe operator working on the new ice pad for the arena had hit a Huron gravesite. "They say there are hundreds of skeletons in there. It would date back hundreds of years. Pretty exciting stuff, eh? I can't believe you haven't heard about it." Courtney was looking down at the frothy foam that had formed on her beer. She didn't notice Jodie's perturbed expression. "Well, I thought you'd be all excited, being part Huron yourself!" Courtney corrected her friend. "Ouendat!"

Courtney had heard Jodie and under different circumstances would have been very excited about the find. She had studied the Ouendats, or Hurons as the French had named them, and her particular interest was derived from the fact that her ancestors on her mother's side were Ouendat from Huronia that included Midland. The story handed down through the generations was that her ancestral grandmother, Strong-Feather, the daughter of the Bear Clan Chief, had become pregnant by a white man and had been forced to leave the community that she had brought great shame on. If she hadn't, she surely would have faced a horrific death at the hands of her intended Iroquois warrior. The Iroquois eventually overtook the peaceful Ouendat nation and slaughtered most of their people, burning their villages to the ground. Strong-Feather ran to escape the certain persecution of the Iroquois. She had also deeply feared the outcome, if she had married into the brutal Iroquois nation. The French explorer, who had impregnated her, took her back to Quebec where she died giving birth to a beautiful baby girl. The child was raised in a culture far from home by the unforgiving family of her ancestral grandfather who, after the death of the baby's mother, took very little interest in the child.

Courtney's actual grandmother had ironically relocated back to Huronia, the home of her ancestoral roots. Courtney's mother had pieced together a history of the family with the help of her mother, and Courtney had enjoyed hearing the stories of her maternal ancestor Strong-Feather that had been handed down through the generations, some of which were probably true, and some probably embellished or even concocted. Jodie interrupted her thoughts.

"Anyway, I just thought it was interesting." Courtney half-heartedly agreed that it was. "So, what's news? How are the wedding plans? Are you getting nervous?" Jodie was leaning in towards Courtney, a huge smile adorning her round red face. Courtney exhaled deeply before she let Jodie know the whole story of what had happened. "Jesus. What the hell is he doing? Have you called him?" The shock in Jodie's voice was still resonating in Courtney's mind. "Of course I've called him! He won't return my calls." Jodie was rummaging through her large purse and eventually pulled out a package of duMaurier cigarettes. Courtney was still focusing on the deep familiar color of the red purse, when she questioned Jodie. "I thought you quit those?" Jodie ignored the question. "What are you going to do, girlfriend?"

Courtney rubbed the back of her head. A nagging headache had formed where she had hit her head earlier. "Well, ... as the wedding will really suck without a groom, I guess I'm going to phone a hundred and fifty people and tell them the whole damn thing is off!" Jodie moved to the edge of her chair. "Like hell! Let him call them!! He's the one responsible for all of this! By the time he's done, his name will be mud in this town!" Jodie quickly dragged on her cigarette exhaling a puff of bluish-gray smoke that floated gently across the patio. Somehow, Courtney doubted that Brad's name would be tarnished by the situation. Almost everyone liked Brad and those that didn't certainly feared him enough not to openly spread rumors. Courtney felt that somehow, like her father would ultimately do, they would blame her. Nothing would stick to Brad. In her mind, she now labeled him the 'Teflon Man'.

"You know I'll do whatever you need done," Jodie offered sympathetically. "I know you will Jodie. Right now I just feel terribly sick over the whole thing. To boot, I'm going over to break the news to mom and dad." The look of concern on Jodie's face made Courtney feel even more squeamish. Jodie offered to come with her. "No. I can do it Jodie. Thanks, anyway." Jodie smiled gently. "Well, how about another beer for courage?" For the first time in three days, Courtney laughed heartily. "It's tempting, but I'd better not. God, but it's so damn tempting!" She stood and hugged her friend who answered back by wrapping her arms around her. "I'll let you know how it goes." Courtney could feel Jodie's sympathetic gaze, as she left the patio.

* * *

Courtney arrived at her parents' house just after seven o'clock, but not before going home to freshen up and check her messages. She was afraid her parents would smell the beer she had with Jodie on her breath. Weighing heavy on her was the guilt she was feeling of not having told them of what had happened. Her parents would certainly admonish her for not having informed them sooner of the situation.

The beautiful old two-story century house stood proud, nestled safely among huge oak trees. A pair of black squirrels ran playfully from one tree to the next. As Courtney proceeded up the long drive, her nervousness increased. She sat parked in the driveway for a moment, in an effort to summon her courage. As she entered the side door of the house, she was greeted by the warm familiar smell of cooking onions. Onion was the main ingredient in her mother's chicken soup. The family recipe had been handed down for generations and was forever deemed the secret to the family's longevity. Even in the heat of summer, there was always a pot of warm chicken soup brewing on the stove. It had, strangely, never seemed odd to Courtney to be cooking soup in the summer.

"Hello Sweetheart," her mother chimed as she entered the kitchen. Her mother kept the house spotless, and yet it had an inviting feeling due to the warm colors and deep rich mahogany trim that wove its way through the house. "Your father is up in the shower. He'll be right down. He was golfing all day. How are the plans going, honey?" Courtney was wondering if she should inform her mother now or wait until both her parents were there together. She decided that having her mother on side would only be to her benefit. "Actually mom, there's been a change in plans." Her mom responded casually. "Oh?" There was no easy way to say what she had to say. "Mom, Brad doesn't want to get married anymore." Her mother was looking at her in stunned silence. It was the same stunned silence Courtney had experienced when Brad had given her the news. It was the same shocked expression that had been on Jodie's face. "What? Oh, no. That's not funny, dear." Her mother could quickly see that Courtney was serious. As the tears began to well up in her daughter's eyes, Eve Myers quickly moved to comfort her only child. "What happened, sweetie?" she whispered. Her arms were now wrapped softly around her crying daughter. "I'm not really sure, mom. He says he's afraid of marriage. He thinks we'll only end up divorced." The tears had turned to sobs as Courtney released the pain she was feeling. "He says he's just not the marrying kind."

 Courtney's mother was still holding her when Doc Myers entered the kitchen. "What's going on here?" The smile on his face had quickly faded when he saw his daughter's tear-streaked face. Courtney's mother didn't skip a beat. "Brad had called off the marriage." Courtney's father stood in the now increasingly familiar shocked disbelief. "What are you talking about? Brad call off the marriage ... that's preposterous!" Courtney was bracing herself for the remainder of her father's retort. "Courtney, what's going on here?" Courtney explained what Brad had said to her three days earlier. "I ... I just simply don't believe it! Why I had lunch with Bill only yesterday. He never mentioned that you and Brad were having difficulties." So Brad had not spilled the news to his parents yet. Courtney had a renewed hope that maybe he was still thinking things through. "Surely Courtney, if this is the case, Brad would have told his parents by now." Courtney caught the slight insinuation that of course Brad would ... but she hadn't. She was bracing herself for further innuendo from her father. "Well, I guess Mr. Perfect isn't so damn perfect anymore! Is he Dad?"

"What the HELL do you mean by that young lady?" Courtney's defenses were working overtime. "What I mean Dad ... is maybe none of us really knew Brad. Maybe we only thought we knew him!" Courtney's father threw up his hands in the air, obviously frustrated. "This is ridiculous!" Turning to his wife, he said, "Eve, have you ever heard of anything as ridiculous as this?" Eve Myers hated these fights. She had been stuck in the middle of her husband's and her daughter's fights for years. Doc Myers continued. "Brad is from good people, Courtney! He wouldn't do this without a damn good reason!" Courtney could feel the hair at the base of her neck start to tingle as her anger mounted. "Well dad, I invite you ... NO, I demand that you find out what that good reason is because quite frankly, I don't believe I've been given one!"

Without hesitation, Doc Myers picked up the phone beside the kitchen table and started dialing the Laduke house. "Oh, hi Marilyn ... Doc Myers calling. Is Bill home?" Doc Myers looked over his glasses at his daughter. "Bill ... hi ... Doc here. Good ... yourself? Yes, uh Bill, the reason I'm calling is we have Courtney here and it seems she's quite upset. Has Brad been around? ... He has! Well, has he mentioned that they are having some difficulties?" Courtney thought that 'difficulties' was a gross understatement. Doc Myers was silent for a long time. "I see. No, she didn't mention that." Courtney's father was looking at her sternly over his glasses that always seemed to be dangling precariously on the end of his nose. Courtney was curious as to what had triggered the look. "Well, of course I don't believe it's true. I think these kids need to get together to try and work this out. Don't you Bill?" There was more silence as Mr. Laduke was once again speaking. "Well, I can understand male pride and all." Doc Myers let a small chuckle escape through his lips. *Male pride and all ... what the hec was he talking about?* "Right ... right ... okay Bill. Yes. I'll talk to her. You too. Bye for now."

As Doc Myers hung up the phone, he pushed his glasses back up his nose with his index finger and looked intently at his daughter. "Courtney, how would you like to tell us everything?" Courtney was totally puzzled by the question. "Dad, I did tell you everything." She despised the disapproving look her father was giving her. "Maybe

YOU'D like to tell ME what's going on, Dad? What did he say?" Doc Myers let out an exhaustive sigh. "Two words, Courtney. Tom Patterson." Tom Patterson was Brad's partner on the local police force and a good friend of Brad's. Courtney's father was waiting for a response from his daughter. "What about Tom Patterson?" Courtney was irritated and puzzled by her father's demeanor and the mention of Brad's partner. "Tom, apparently, told Brad that you made a play for him." Shock swept over Courtney. "Well, that's the first time I've heard of that dad and it's simply not true! I'm no more interested in Tom Patterson than fly!" Her father was still looking sternly at her. "Well Courtney, did you tell that to Brad?" Courtney's father just wasn't getting it and Courtney felt frustrated. "Dad, I never talked to Brad about Tom Patterson, because nothing ever happened between us, and Tom and Brad damn well know that!" Doc Myers was silent for a moment. "Well, then someone is lying!" Courtney exploded in anger. "Yes! Dad! Someone is lying and it damn well isn't me!" She wished at that moment that her father would say something to confirm that he believed that it wasn't her that was lying, but he didn't.

Courtney got up quickly from the kitchen table. "Mom," she said kissing her mother on the cheek. "I've got to go." Eve Myers' eyes were pleading for Courtney to stay. "I'm sorry, mom." Courtney turned to her father. "Dad ... Tom and I ... that is absolutely beyond ridiculous! I loved Brad and only Brad, and I shouldn't be standing here defending something that just never, ever happened." Doc Myers was slowly being swayed by the intensity of his daughter's words, but it was too late. Courtney slammed the screen door behind her and ran for her car. She vaguely heard the screen door creak open. No doubt her father was standing on the porch yelling after her. She refused to look back. The anger that now totally engulfed her mind had blocked out his beckoning as she sped away.

* * *

Courtney drove for half an hour until she reached the white sandy beaches of Nottawasaga Bay. As a teenager, Courtney and her friends would often ride their bikes to the popular Balm Beach. It was a hangout for young people mostly due to the arcade and waterside restaurant that had been there long before Courtney was born. Although it wasn't 'her' place, it was beautiful nonetheless and she had spent a great deal of time there over the years. The sun was just setting in the distance, seemingly extinguishing itself in the dark water. She slipped off her sandals and walked barefoot to the water's edge. Courtney stared out across the darkening blueness, as she had done many times before. "What the hell!" she yelled angrily against the crashing of the waves. A couple further down the beach turned trying to focus on who was yelling, and then continued on their way.

Either Bill Laduke was lying, or Brad had lied, or Tom Patterson had lied, or they had all conspired to lie in an effort to save Brad's reputation. Sure, if it looked like she was the one who caused the relationship to end, then Brad would save face in their small town. In the end, she would be made to look like the bad one. It would be her reputation that would be tarnished. She couldn't imagine Tom Patterson coming up with this all by himself. Although she didn't particularly mind him, he had no designs on her, or she on him. Quite frankly, Courtney had never thought of him as the sharpest tool in the shed. They were casual acquaintances but nothing more. She had thought he was one of those guys with too much brawn and not enough brains and she had often wondered how he had ever managed to become a police officer. No, the formation of the lie had to be between Brad and his father. She became even angrier with her father for having given credence to Brad and his father's version of events. "I just have to get away from here!" Seething with anger, Courtney turned and walked quickly back to her car. The pain in the back of her head had intensified to the point that she walked huddled with one hand covering the now chronic throbbing. She wiped away the angry tears with her other hand. "Damn him!" she exclaimed.

* * *

On her way home, she passed Little Lake Park and saw the newly erected sign for the building of the arena pad. Her car turned into the park. She felt eerily like a passenger who had no say in the direction she was traveling. Passing through the pine tree lined entranceway; she saw the small lake on her right hand side. The water was smooth. The car parked itself in front of the small white building that was labeled in bright red painted letters, 'Dobbie's'. The French fry stand was just closing for the night and Courtney watched as the owner closed and locked the front doors to the building. She had, as a teenager, worked there for one summer peeling potatoes outside the back door of the store. It was named 'Johnny's' at that time. Johnny and his wife had made the French fries famous, but eventually sold the business when they became too old to manage it. Dobbie's continued the famous heavily salted peanut oil fried potatoes that had been served at that location for decades. Tourists would still line up for a chance to taste the greasy delicacies.

The owner of the store appeared from behind the building and got in a beat-up old red pick-up truck. Driving slowly past Courtney's car, she could sense his look and busied herself by pretending to look for something in the car's glove box. After a few seconds, she looked up and could see the truck disappearing behind the rows of pine trees up the hill.

The park was unusually quiet, as Courtney left the sanctity of her car. It was unusual not to see anyone in the park and there was a strange calmness as the darkness of night quickly approached. For a second, she wondered, *Where are the birds?* There were always seagulls hanging around the store waiting for a dropped greasy morsel or two. Even the water of the lake was devoid of the large number of Canada Geese that arrived and overtook the beach this time of year. Courtney could see that the road ahead was blocked. The only way to proceed was on foot and, once again, Courtney felt powerless as she began to walk up the steep hill towards the arena construction site. Each step became increasingly difficult. It felt like some unseen energy was trying to stop Courtney from continuing. She struggled on, determined to see whatever she had come for.

The construction site was larger than Courtney had expected. As she stepped over the yellow caution tape that pathetically secured the site, she proceeded down to the sandy base. There was no denying an ominous feeling as Courtney stood on what was intended to be the eventual ice-pad. The game of ice hockey had been historically recorded as invented by the Ouendats, and not by modern Canadians as was usually claimed. Ouendat or Huron boys played with curved sticks, sliding over the snow, hitting a ball made of wood. Courtney thought of the irony of the situation. Buried on the arena site would

THE RED MASK

be the remains of some of the young Indians who had once played the game.

"Hey!! What the hec are you doing down there?" Courtney could see the shadowy image of a woman at the top of the hill. "Get out of there ... right now!" Courtney was shocked that she wasn't alone and sheepishly ascended out of the site. As she approached the figure, she could see the security uniform adorning the rather large woman. "I'm ... I'm sorry. I didn't know." Courtney did know however, that the site was off limits, as she had crossed the yellow caution tape without a second thought. "What were you doing down there?" The stern looking woman was demanding an answer. Courtney didn't want to tell the woman how she had been summoned to the site by some inexplicable force. She continued to stand stupefied in front of the large woman. "I ... I was just out for a walk." The guard was not fooled. "Oh, you're one of them." Courtney looked at the guard somewhat puzzled. She wanted to ask to whom the guard was referring, but remained silent. "Either you leave, or I'll call the police."

Courtney began to panic. The last thing she needed was for Brad to turn up and find her in this predicament. "I'm going. My car is down at Dobbie's." Courtney could feel the guard's eyes burrowing into her back as she left. Courtney now saw the wooden structure that had been built into the side of the slope. Her body turned icy cold, as she looked at the structure. *They're in there,* she thought.

* * *

Arriving back at the apartment, she checked her phone messages. There was only one from her mother. "Courtney ... honey ... your father and I are quite worried about you. Please call when you get in. Your father feels really bad about the way he acted. Please, honey. Call us back." Courtney quickly erased the message. "You feel so bad; you couldn't call yourself, eh dad?" Still, the obvious concern in her mother's voice had somewhat softened her anger.

She dialed the Laduke house and was surprised when Bill Laduke answered the phone. "Uh, Mr. Laduke. It's Courtney. Is Brad there? I need to speak to him!" Bill Laduke hesitantly said he would check. Courtney waited for what seemed an eternity. "What do you want,

Courtney?" Brad's voice exuded arrogance. Courtney was a little taken aback by the lack of feeling and stinging tone of his greeting. "Well, to start with Brad, I would like some explanation as to the lies that are surfacing about my involvement with Tom Patterson!" Silence followed. "Brad! Damn it, Brad! Answer me!" Brad cleared his throat, but didn't respond. "Brad. You lied to your parents!" Courtney was now thinking that it was Brad who had concocted the story and it hurt her deeply. "Why are you doing this to me?" Brad finally spoke. "Look Courtney. I'm sorry you feel this way, but Tom told me everything." Courtney was beyond angry. "Tom told you nothing! You're a real jerk for not facing up to the fact that it is you who is responsible for this whole thing falling apart. What did you promise Tom, Brad? Tell me! What did it take? It probably wasn't much more than a case of beer or a bottle of rye, and for that you're willing to ruin my reputation?" For a moment, Brad was silent. "Look Courtney. I'm not interested in spending my life with a woman who's not faithful." Courtney was now clutching the phone with both hands. "Oh, give me a break Brad! Is your dad there? Is that who you're trying to fool? You're pathetic, and to think I thought I knew you! I thought you were the one! I thought you were made of something! I gave everything I had to you!"

Courtney slammed down the receiver. Grabbing the two decorative pillows off of the couch, she flung them furiously across the room in opposing directions. Running to her closet, she pulled out the garbage bag of things she had collected, and dragged it out of the apartment and down to the large blue dumpster in the back of the building. Struggling to throw the bag into the tall metal container, she yelled, "Good riddance Brad ... you jerk!" The bag hit the bottom of the empty dumpster creating a hollow bang. Courtney stood mesmerized by the sound. She felt so terribly alone.

Chapter 2

The sign above the entrance to 'Charlie's' read:

> *'The Lord in his goodness, sent the grape,*
> *To Cheer both great and small,*
> *Sometimes little fools drink too much,*
> *And great fools not at all!'*

—*Anonymous*

* * *

The days passed slowly into weeks until the ominous day that should have been Courtney and Brad's wedding. It was almost one o'clock in the morning. Courtney was just finishing work at Charlie's when a fight broke out in the bar, a typical occurrence at the end of the night in the small town bar. As things escalated between the parties involved, and the situation became increasingly out of control, Courtney's boss, Jeff, was forced to call the police. Brad Laduke and Tom Patterson were dispatched to deal with the situation. After their arrival, things did indeed settle down. Jeff called taxis to take the intoxicated participants to their homes.

Courtney's heart was beating rapidly at the sight of Brad. Despite the lump that had formed in her throat, she managed a cool, non-emotional "Hello, Brad." Brad was looking at her with a slight look of irritation. His acknowledgement was a curt nod and there was fake disdain evident with the returned greeting. Courtney became agitated with the obvious performance. "Look Brad, if you and Tom have a moment, I'd like to speak with you both." Courtney was gesturing towards a secluded booth at the back of the bar. She desperately wanted to hear what Tom had to say in Brad's presence.

"No. I don't think so." Brad then mumbled something under his breath. It had sounded to Courtney like, "This has been hard enough on me." Courtney cleared the nervous lump from her throat. "Excuse me. What did you say? I thought I heard that this has been hard enough on YOU!" Brad's eyes shot around the bar. "You must be joking, Brad. You and your buddy have tarnished my reputation with your lies. I thought you were more of a man than to lie about your own lack of commitment. You had no right to do this to me, Brad!" Courtney's voice had risen making it audible to the few remaining patrons and staff.

"Hey Tom! How about it!" Courtney was yelling across the bar in Tom Patterson's direction but her eyes were firmly planted on Brad. Tom Patterson was looking nervously around the bar knowing he was in a difficult situation. "I'll be in the cruiser, Brad," he said exiting the bar. Courtney continued her venomous attack on Brad. "Are you so afraid of what your Daddy will think of you Brad that you have to hide behind some cock and bull story?" Brad's anger was mounting due to his embarrassment. "Look. This is neither the time or the place." Courtney let out an angry laugh. "Sure. Of course! You're right. Maybe we could do lunch and discuss what a total jerk you are!" Brad turned quickly on the polished heel of his shoe and made his way towards the exit. Fists clenched in frustration, Courtney stood and watched as the man she had so desperately loved, and given of herself so freely, walked away on this of all days. All remaining eyes were on her. "Show's over folks," Jeff announced to the remaining patrons. He placed an arm around Courtney's shoulder and ushered her to the secluded booth.

"I'm ... I'm so sorry Jeff." Jeff smiled gently at Courtney and patted her hand. "Frankly, I'm not sure what took you so long?" Courtney looked forlornly at her boss. "Courtney, I'm going to give you some unsolicited advice. I want you to take tomorrow night off and sit and really think about what it is you want to do with your life. You'll rot here and there's so much more you're capable of. Brad will make your life miserable and you're too pretty of a girl to wear such a bitter face." Courtney forced a smile. "So. You think I should just run away?" Jeff smiled back at his friend. "No. I think you

THE RED MASK

should go find a new life. You should go and find some happiness for yourself. God knows, you won't find it here." Courtney thought that maybe Jeff was right. Maybe a change and a challenge would be good. "I'll think about it Jeff ... and I will take tomorrow night off. Thanks!" Jeff squeezed Courtney's hand and then slowly moved his hand away and returned to the bar where he started cleaning up for the next day. As much as Courtney enjoyed working at the bar, she recognized that Jeff was probably right. Staying in this town held no future for her.

* * *

Courtney couldn't sleep that night for thinking about the way Brad had just walked away from her in the bar. Jeff's suggestion about starting her life over somewhere else haunted her thoughts. She knew Jeff was right about how staying would just bring back the bitterness she felt towards Brad. She thought about how her parents had called all of their guests to tell them that the wedding was off and the surprise they must all have felt. She thought of the monumental task of returning all of the shower gifts. Although all of their friends said they understood, she wondered what they were saying behind their doors. It had all hurt her so deeply and she now despised Brad. She hated him as passionately as she had once loved him. He had introduced her to a feeling that she despised; and she wanted to relinquish it. Her true enemy was now within, and she wanted desperately to eliminate the bitterness she felt in her soul.

Courtney took stock of her skills. She had been an honors graduate at college and really had been looking forward to working in the hospitality field. She knew she would have to start at the bottom and gradually work her way up in the industry, as working at Charlie's was her only hospitality experience. She thought about Toronto. The thought of the big city scared her. She had visited there over the years, but had never had any real desire to live there. With meager savings, she worried about how she would even afford to relocate. The city would be a much more expensive prospect. She thought about asking her parents for help, but knew they would disapprove immediately about her moving so far away. They would definitely not accept her moving to Toronto.

As she sat up on the side of her bed, a frustrated energy burned deep in her soul and shot through to her fingertips. She closed her eyes in an attempt to calm herself, but an increasingly familiar flash of red shot in front of her closed lids. The blood red color was haunting. Attempting to calm herself, she decided that a cup of tea might help. As she made her way to the kitchen to boil the kettle for the tea, a sudden hammering at the door startled her.

She remained trapped in her steps for a few seconds. The clock read that it was nearly four o'clock in the morning! She couldn't imagine who would come calling at this ridiculous hour. As she tiptoed silently to the door and peeked through the peephole, she saw the distorted image of Brad. Courtney stood frozen, wondering what she should do. Brad's manner answered the question. "Open the damn door! Courtney! I know you're in there!" The slur in Brad's words meant he had been drinking. "I want my stuff! Open the bloody door ... now!!" Courtney was afraid of the tone in his voice, but it wasn't like she could call the police. Brad resumed the pounding, the sound resonating through the entire apartment. An icy tingle moved through her body as she stood in fear. Covering her ears to block out the sound, she silently begged God to make him stop. "Fine. I'll be back tomorrow for my things ... oh, and I want the damn ring back!" Courtney could hear silence in the hallway but knew intuitively he was still there ... waiting. She tiptoed into the bedroom and threw on jeans and a sweatshirt. If he forced his way in, she wanted to be, at the very least, dressed. Courtney had never experienced this side of Brad, or any man for that matter. She had never imagined he could be like this.

Returning to within feet of the man she had once loved, she listened intently. She decided to slide a kitchen chair under the knob of the front door, being careful not to disturb the doorknob in the process. This was a difficult task, given the fact that her hands were now shaking. After a few minutes, the pounding resumed. Courtney was tempted to yell, but knew that would only confirm that she was indeed in the apartment. He had probably already checked to see if her car was parked in the back lot behind the drugstore. *"Oh God,"* she thought. *"Don't do anything to my car?"* Courtney debated as to what to do. She took the cordless phone into the bathroom and dialed the Laduke house.

THE RED MASK

After several rings, Bill Laduke finally answered the phone. "I'm sorry to disturb you at this hour." Courtney's call was reciprocated by a gruff, "What the hell do you want? Do you have any idea of the time, young lady?" Courtney went on to explain the situation. "Please, I'm afraid to open the door. Please ... please, I'm begging you. Please, come and get him." Mr. Laduke hesitantly agreed to come.

After another ten minutes, and repeated sporadic attempts by Brad to get Courtney to open the door, Courtney could hear Bill Laduke in the hallway outside of her apartment. "Come on son, time to go home." Brad was slurring his words. "She's ... she's got my stuff, dad." Brad sounded like a little boy that had a favorite toy taken away. Courtney hated him more than ever, as she listened to his pathetic appeals. Mr. Laduke responded loud enough for Courtney to hear. "Okay. Okay son, I spoke to Courtney and I'll get your stuff in the morning. Come on now, get up." Brad was obviously sitting in the hallway, probably too drunk to continue standing. Courtney could hear the older man straining to lift his intoxicated son. "Now, now, she's not worth all this." Once again, the words were clearly meant for Courtney to hear and they hurt her deeply. As she heard the pair struggle down the stairs, Courtney quickly went and grabbed her suitcase from the hall closet. The tears were streaming down her face and she wrestled with the intense disappointment she felt. She had loved not only Brad, but also his family. She realized that they were blaming her for the failure of the relationship. She vowed she would never trust any man again!

Courtney worked until dawn packing up as many things as she could fit into her small car. The major furniture, such as it was, would have to stay. She had three weeks left on this month's rent and she had also paid an additional month to secure the apartment. She was hopeful that she would be settled somewhere in the next three weeks, so she could give formal notice. After throwing the spare key Brad had left to the apartment on the kitchen table, she closed the apartment door behind her. She drove in a zombie-like state to the city and at this point was totally exhausted by all that had happened. Somewhere on the west side of Toronto, near Lake Ontario, she pulled into a park. She reclined her seat and closed her eyes. "She felt alone, but safe."

* * *

Courtney's dreams were of the night before. Brad was pounding on the door. "Courtney. I know you're in there. Let me in or I'll kill you!" Brad had transformed into a creature from a time long ago. He wore a mask with long thick horse-like hair. The eyes were hollow black spaces that looked deep within her. "Bang, bang, bang!" Courtney awoke with a start and jumped as the face of a police officer glared through her driver side window. The hollow black spaces had been replaced by piercing blue eyes. They seemed to be looking right through her.

His words were muffled. Shakily, she struggled to roll down the driver side window. "Miss ... you can't stay here." Courtney, still obviously startled, could sense that the stranger felt guilty for having woken her. "I'm sorry. You've been here for over four hours." Courtney struggled for words. The sight of the police uniform had somewhat stupefied her. "I'm sorry. I must have fallen asleep. I ... I was dreaming." The police officer was surveying her overly packed car. "Are you going somewhere?" Still authoritative, his tone had softened slightly. "Yes," she answered honestly. "I'm new here. I'm going to look for a place to live." The officer seemed a little intrigued. "Where are you going to look?" She told him she had no idea. "As I said, I'm new here. I don't really even know where to start looking?"

"I'll be right back." She watched as the officer walked to the cruiser parked behind her car. He returned, after a few seconds, with a map in his hand. "You can get out of the car. I won't bite." Courtney could tell that he sensed her trepidation. Reluctantly, she got out of the sanctity of her car. The officer made her feel small. Courtney was five foot four inches tall and she guessed that the policeman was nearly a foot taller. He bent awkwardly to open the map on the hood of the small car. "Okay. You're here," he said pointing to a spot on the left side of the map. "Are you familiar with the city at all?" Although she did know a bit from her previous visits to the city, Courtney indicated that she wasn't. "The city is really a quilt of many different communities."

He pointed to the downtown, Chinatown, the Greek area called the Danforth, Little Italy, and the west side called Etobicoke.

"You're in south Etobicoke now." He continued to explain how everything was accessible by transit and no matter where you were, you could be where you wanted to be fairly quickly. Courtney was looking at the officer with doe-eyed wonder. "Okay, look. As you are new here, can I make a suggestion? I know of some smaller low-rise apartments not far from here. I know they have vacancies. They're not the greatest, but they're clean and fairly reasonable." The tall, handsome police officer had said the magic word. "Why don't you follow me up there? Oh, and by the way, my name is Jack ... Jack O'Brien." Courtney extended her trembling hand to shake the officer's. Her hand felt very small in his. "Courtney," she nervously answered back, not offering her last name.

And so it was, Courtney had a police escort to a series of low-rise apartments located minutes from the park. Her nervousness had permeated through her entire body and she had to apply the brake quite hard when the cruiser stopped at a red light in front of her. She could see the eyes of the stranger looking at her in his rear view mirror. She knew he was wondering what her story was? As they continued on, she didn't have to look to know that he was still watching her. She struggled to focus more diligently on the taillights of the cruiser. The policeman finally slowed in front of an older, white, three-story apartment building. The front of the building appeared well kept and Courtney noted the bright yellow chrysanthemums that lined the gardens up the front walkway.

The sign on the front lawn of the building simply said 'one bedroom'. As the cruiser slowly continued into the parking lot behind the building, Courtney followed and parked her car in the spot behind it. Jack O'Brien was at her door before she had a chance to exit the car. "It's one of the nicer buildings in the neighborhood and the bus stop is right out front." He walked Courtney back around to the front lobby and buzzed the button beside the label that read 'Superintendent'. "We rarely get calls here." Courtney assumed that he was inferring that the people who lived there were decent, law-abiding types.

The Superintendent seemed surprised to see a police officer waiting in the lobby. He was a small Italian looking man. "We're here to see the apartment that you are advertising for rent." The superintendent looked relieved. He led Courtney and her now police escort to the second floor and stopped in front of a door with the number 212 stuck on it with black peel and stick numbers. As the door opened, Courtney was shocked by the size of the apartment. The superintendent said in somewhat broken English, "My wife, Maria, she just clean. She do nice job. Sometimes …". The superintendent waved his hands in the air in circular motions indicating that sometimes the apartments were left a mess.

The apartment had a large eat-in kitchen, a huge central room with a balcony, a smaller bedroom, and a decent size bathroom with bright blue and orange fish wallpaper. The wallpaper made Courtney smile. As she turned, she could see that the Police Officer was smiling too. For a second, their eyes connected in a strange way and Courtney could feel the heat rush to her cheeks. "How much is it?" Jack O'Brien had taken over the conversation. "Cheap, cheap … only six hundred fifty. We have the rent review." Courtney didn't really know what 'rent review' was, and she looked questioningly at the officer. "They only put the rent up minimally each year, maybe three percent. But when a tenant moves out, the owner is allowed to increase it substantially. Depending on how long a tenant stays, you could have two identical apartments at vastly different rents." He turned to the Superintendent. "When is it available?" The Superintendent told him it would be ready the following week. "We'd like it now … today." The Superintendent hesitated for a moment. "I don't know. The rent, it monthly." Jack O'Brien was undaunted by the small man's hesitation. "Well, you could just prorate it. I would assume the owner would like to rent it, as opposed to having it sit vacant?" The Superintendent bowed to the authoritative tone of the officer's voice. "Okay. I need you to fill out the application. You both be listed." The policeman jumped in immediately. "The apartment is just for my cousin." Courtney couldn't believe how easily the lie came from the man's mouth, but she didn't interfere with the discussion. Her heart was beating so hard in her chest, she was certain both men could hear it. "Okay, I be back."

As the superintendent left the apartment, Courtney looked up at the uniformed man beside her. "Cousin?" The man, she didn't even know an hour before, laughed. "I hope you like the place. It looks like it's yours." Courtney smiled gratefully. "I do like it. I really do.

I can't tell you how much I appreciate your help. You've certainly gone beyond the call of duty ... ". The stranger filled in the blank. "Jack. Call me Jack." Just then the superintendent returned with the necessary paperwork. "I have to get back to work. I'll be back at five, to make sure you're okay?" Although surprised that he would be back, Courtney was also a little relieved. After he left, she settled the financial arrangement of first and last month's rent and the prorated amount for the extra week. The superintendent, who now introduced himself as Joe, told her to let him know when the furniture would be arriving. "There's only one elevator and there's lots of old people in the building who need it."

Courtney thought about her pathetic furniture at the other apartment. The kitchen set, which included four duct-taped chairs, could certainly stay where it was. She had hated the set that she had inherited with the apartment. "Actually," she said, "I would like to purchase a new kitchen set. Is there a mall near here?" The superintendent gave Courtney directions to a large shopping mall about five minutes from the building. Before leaving, he gave her a pair of shiny silver keys for the apartment. After thanking him, she stood alone. "I like it." She had been trying to convince herself that the move to the big city was the right one. The rent was almost double what she had paid back home, and with no income, she was worried about how she would manage. Courtney had already dipped into her savings substantially with the rent check, but knew if she was frugal with the money she had left, she could afford a small kitchen set.

She ran down to her car with a slight bounce in her step. There was an increasing excitement about her new apartment and her new life. It took several trips to bring all of the things that were in her car up to the apartment. She opened the fridge half expecting that there would be some food in it. She thought she had better find out where a grocery store was.

She ran into Joe, as she headed for the elevator. Courtney asked about a grocery store. He told her there was one just down the hill behind the apartment building. Courtney thought it was great that she could walk there in a pinch. She would drive to the mall first and then venture out to find the grocery store. She thanked the superintendent again, and left her 'new 'building.

* * *

The sprawling mall was one of the biggest Courtney had ever seen. As she entered the large anchor department store, she didn't know where to begin looking for furniture. Unlike the one-level department store she was used to in Midland, the store had many floors. She located a store directory at the base of the escalators and headed up to the top floor where the furniture section was housed. Courtney couldn't remember the last time she was on an escalator and she gingerly stepped onto the moving silver staircase holding firmly to the black rubber railing. Once on the top floor, she looked through the vast array of kitchen and dining room sets that, although exquisite, were totally out of her price range. "Can I help you?" An older well-dressed saleslady was approaching. "Well, quite honestly, I think what you have in kitchen sets is a little out of my price range. I just wanted something small and inexpensive." The saleslady looked thoughtful. "If you don't mind a little scratch and dent, I may have something for you? We were just going to ship it out to the clearance center." The friendly saleslady led Courtney through two double doors at the back of the showroom.

Tucked away in the back corner of the furniture receiving area was a lovely wicker set that consisted of a small glass-topped table and two smaller wicker chairs that tucked neatly underneath it. Courtney fell in love with it immediately. "What's wrong with it?" she asked looking for some sign of imperfection. The saleslady studied the tag affixed to one of the chairs. "Well, one of the table legs has a scratch on it." There was indeed a deep scratch on one of the legs. "If you get one of those furniture markers, you won't even notice it." The saleslady continued to look at the tag affixed to the chair. "Oh, and one of the chair pads apparently has a rip in the seam." The lady found the imperfection. "Nothing a needle and thread won't fix." Courtney liked the delicate green and pink colors of the chair pads. They added to the tropical look of the set. She looked at the discounted price below the original price on the tag ... $599. That was almost an entire month's rent. "Oh. Gosh, no. I doubt I can afford this?" The saleslady appeared undaunted. "What were you looking to spend?" Courtney told her she was thinking maybe three hundred. She knew that even three hundred dollars would be stretching her budget. "I don't think we can go that low, but I'll ask. If you don't ask, you don't get. I'll be right back."

Left alone beside the kitchen set, Courtney once again looked the small set up and down. As she stood up, the breath suddenly left her body. Leaning against the wall, behind a bedroom set, was a familiar framed print. Her mother had the same print hanging in the living room of the family's home. The print was of the face of an Ouendat Chief standing in front of an Ouendat longhouse. Courtney knew she had to have it.

"Well, you caught him in a good mood. It's yours for three hundred!" Courtney, once again, looked the kitchen set over. She knew it was an incredible deal, but felt the guilt of spending money. She was thinking that she would just have to give up on luxuries ... like food. "Will you be taking it with you or would you like it delivered? It's fifty dollars for delivery." The saleslady must have realized that Courtney was on an extremely tight budget and that another fifty dollars would be totally out of the question. Courtney did appreciate, however, that the lady had been polite enough to ask. She didn't hesitate. "I'll be taking it with me." The saleslady smiled softly at the young girl. "That print over there ... how much is it?" The saleslady walked Courtney over to the print. "It's a hundred and fifty." There was no hesitation this time. "I'll take it, too!" The saleslady looked at her with surprise and then what appeared to be a hint of perturbed mistrust.

* * *

Courtney waited at the delivery dock for her new kitchen set to make its appearance from behind the thick black doors of the freight elevator. It took nearly an hour. She was thankful that the top of the table came off of the wicker base. After carefully loading the table and picture in her trunk, she managed to squeeze the two chairs into the backseat of her car. She knew she never would have managed a larger set.

Back at her apartment, she decided to let Joe know that she would be bringing the set up in the elevator. He offered his help, which Courtney graciously accepted. Courtney was a little embarrassed that she had just thrown all of the things from her car in the center of the kitchen, but Joe didn't seem to notice. "Thank you. You're very kind." The superintendent looked pleased that he could help. "Okay, okay. Just let me know when the rest is coming. You got a screwdriver to fix that top?" Joe was pointing at the glass tabletop with the taped bag of screws affixed to it. Courtney thought for a second. "No, actually, I don't." Joe offered to get one from his apartment. He was turning out to be quite a nice person. Not only did he get the screwdriver, but he also reattached the tabletop. "Thanks again, Joe." He surveyed his handiwork. "It nice," he said referring to the set. "It got a scratch though." Courtney pretended to be shocked. "Oh no. I must have done that loading it in my car." She gently ran a finger over the deep scratch on the table leg. She wasn't sure why she didn't want Joe to know that she had bargain shopped for the table and chairs. She was glad that the store had taken off the discounted tag and stapled it to her bill. The nice man also helped her hang the picture on the wall above the table, but didn't comment on the drawing of the Indian. Courtney surmised that it simply didn't appeal to him.

After Joe left, Courtney sat on one of the chairs at her new kitchen table. She looked at the picture of the Indian chief and spoke to him as if he was real. "I really like this. I don't have bed, but I have a great kitchen set!" Courtney searched through the boxes on the kitchen floor to find the small black metal tin that housed her needles and thread. Her mother had given it to her when she moved into the apartment in Midland. As she ran her hand over the faded drawing of a peacock on the lid of the tin, she suddenly realized how much she missed her mother. As tempted as she was to call her, she knew she needed to settle the idea of the move in her own mind first.

Sitting at the new table, Courtney mended the ripped chair pad. She had brought an air mattress for the interim, until she could make arrangements to get her bed. Realizing that she hadn't eaten anything since the previous day, she decided to look through the box and cooler that she had brought from the old apartment. The grocery store would have to wait, as she was now feeling exhausted from the day. She wiped out the cupboards before unpacking the box of dry goods. Although the apartment was indeed clean, she felt better giving the cupboards a wipe herself. She put on some chicken noodle soup while she continued to unpack. "So, how do you like it?" she asked the proud man in the picture. "Yes. It is nice, isn't it?" The soft eyes of the Ouendat chief seemed to be looking at her compassionately. Courtney knew an artist had just created him from his imagination, but the Indian looked so real to her. Her thoughts traveled away from the picture and back to the task at hand.

Courtney spent the balance of the afternoon unpacking the array of items she had brought. She put her small CD player on the kitchen counter and searched the channels of the radio until she found the soft, soothing music of Sarah Brightman. A loud noise filled the kitchen, shocking her peaceful surroundings. She realized it was the buzz from the intercom. She awkwardly pushed the speak button and said "Hello?" She then pushed the listen button. "Hey, it's me Jack." Courtney nervously buzzed Jack O'Brien in. The clock on the stove read exactly 'five o'clock'. A moment later he was at the door.

The change of his attire caught her off guard. He was dressed in a pair of faded Levi's and cream-colored shirt. She couldn't help but notice that he was a handsome man. The strength of his body had been hidden in his uniform. He obviously spent time working out. Courtney had always felt that guys that spent a lot of time on their bodies were either conceited or the opposite, basically insecure and trying to compensate by developing their bodies. It was not her intent to find out which of these Jack O'Brien was. He was a man, and a cop, and that was two strikes against him. Still, she had noticed his body and that troubled her.

"Nice kitchen set." He then stood and surveyed the print, but offered no initial opinion on it. "Thanks. Glad you like it. It's the only furniture I have!" Courtney's nervousness was apparent in her laugh. "Well, it's more than you had this morning." Jack O'Brien sat gingerly on one of the wicker chairs. Courtney was relieved that the chair seemed to withstand his weight just fine. Although uncomfortable with his presence, she continued to notice just how handsome he was. His smile was infectious. Laugh lines surrounded his deep blue eyes and the lines told Courtney that he was a man who enjoyed life and had laughed a lot over the years. Traces of a dark shadow of a beard seemed to accentuate the piercing blue of his eyes. It was his eyes that had initially caught her off guard in the parking lot earlier that day. "I like the picture," he finally said matter-of-factly.

"Yes. So do I." Courtney hesitated, wondering if she should elaborate on why she had bought the print. "You like Indians do you?" Courtney smiled. "Yes. I have Ouendat roots." He didn't seem surprised by the information. "Oh, so you are a Huron." Courtney was perturbed by Jack's usage of the French term for Ouendat. It had always bothered her when the word Huron was used. Her mother had instilled in her a hatred for the term. She remembered one particularly bad fight between her parents in which her father referred to her mother as a 'dumb Huron'. Her normally passive mother had thrown a cup of coffee across the room and yelled fiercely at her father to never call her 'dumb' or 'Huron' again. It had been the angriest she had ever seen her mother. Courtney quickly changed the subject.

"Can I get you a coffee ... tea ... anything?" Jack told her that a tea would be fine. "I drink way too much coffee. Listen ... I need to run down to my car for a moment." Courtney was curious as to why he had to run down to his car, but said she would make the tea while he was gone. After buzzing Jack back in, she nearly fell over when he re-entered the apartment with a huge palm like plant. "What the hec?" she said in disbelief. Jack said he hoped she didn't mind, but he had bought her a housewarming gift. "Where do you want it?" he said peaking out from behind the leaves. She nervously pointed to the living room. She was still in shock that a relative stranger had purchased a gift for someone that they barely knew. She was now starting to question his motives. Men were, after all, snakes that struck their prey before devouring them.

Jack was surveying the large plant that he had placed by the sliding doors leading to the balcony. He had a pleased expression on his face. "Look ... Jack." Courtney's stomach was in knots as she spoke. "The gift is really very nice, but just so we're clear about things; I'm not looking for any sort of relationship right now." Jack was now looking at her with a slightly astonished expression. "Oh, God. I'm sorry. I'm not looking for a relationship either. As a matter of fact, I have a girlfriend. It's just that you looked so lost when I found you this morning. I was just trying to say, well ... welcome." Courtney relaxed a bit and now felt a little silly about the assumption. "I'm sorry. I guess I assumed too much behind your gesture. I just figured that people don't do things unless they expect something in return." Jack O'Brien smiled down at her. "That's okay. It's okay to be suspicious. You're in the big city now." Her mistrust of Brad now lumped all men in the same category. She couldn't help the cautiousness she felt towards another man and especially another police officer. She knew there was a brotherhood between cops and she suspected he wouldn't believe her story if she told it to him.

Still, Courtney continued to feel quite badly that she had jumped to a conclusion about this man. She served him his cup of tea and sat down at the kitchen table with him. "Well, this is my first time using my new kitchen set." He was smiling at her. "So, what brought you here?" Courtney had rehearsed the lie, but the question had still taken her breath away. "Well, I graduated from Georgian in Hospitality and Tourism. There aren't too many jobs in my field up where I'm from in Midland. I decided to move to the big city and see if I could land a job in my field." She knew he was thinking that it was just too neat ... too rehearsed. "What does your family think of your move?" Courtney wasn't expecting the question. "Oh, they think it's great. I have their total blessing." A slight hint of sarcasm had crept into her voice and she wondered if he had picked up on it. "A pretty girl like you must have a boyfriend?" Courtney blushed at the compliment, but wished he would just stop asking her questions. "I've had my share, but none presently." Jack smiled a devilish smile that seemed to have a strange affect on her. "Well, I'm sure that will change." The engagement ring on Courtney's finger had not gone unnoticed.

Jack and Courtney talked for a while about the city. He recommended several big name hotels in the heart of the city that he felt were worth Courtney's time investigating. Finally, he thanked her for the tea and got up to leave. "I'd like to check in from time to time to make sure you're okay?" Courtney agreed that it would be nice if he did, but secretly wished he wouldn't. What else could she say? He had been so very kind. "Thanks again for everything; the apartment ... the plant. You've been really great!" As she opened the door he said, "Glad to help." He was finally gone. Courtney couldn't help but let out a huge sigh of relief. She hoped that was the end of Jack O'Brien.

* * *

Courtney spent the balance of the evening arranging her closet, blowing up the air mattress that would serve as her bed, and wondering how she was going to tell her parents about the move. She didn't have a telephone, so she decided that first thing the next day she would call them from a pay phone and let them know that she was safe. She knew they would be worried about the move, but she didn't want them to fear the worst. She also knew that she was taking the coward's way out, as her parents would not be home during the day, and she could simply leave a message on their answering machine. She wasn't ready to hear her father's negative reaction to the move. He would berate her, and the thought of it caused her to feel sick in the depth of her stomach.

Courtney was also trying to imagine the Laduke's reaction to her move. She remembered Bill Laduke saying to Brad that he would come back in the morning for Brad's things. She wondered if he had come that morning. She twisted the engagement ring off of her finger, placing it on her right hand. She now hated the ring, but had continued to wear it for fear of losing it. Brad could have the stupid thing back, for all she cared. It meant nothing to her now. She planned to return it by giving it to Jodie or her parents the next time she saw them. They could drop it off at the Laduke's, as she had no desire to ever see them again.

As she thought about how much had happened since the evening before at her old apartment, she began to feel very tired. Other than the few hours sleep she had got at the park that morning, Courtney had no chance to rest. She thought about how Brad would be angry when he discovered that she had thrown out all of his things, but she also had a custom made wedding dress that she would definitely never wear and so her guilt was quickly eroding.

As she slipped into her sleeping bag on the makeshift bed, she could feel her eyes wearily close. She could hear the muffled noises in the apartments surrounding hers. The steady sound of cars passing by the apartment did not affect her ability to go to sleep. She was used to the sound of traffic on the main street outside her apartment in Midland. "It's going to be okay," she whispered. "I'm going to make it here! I need to make it here! There's no going back!" Strangely, she felt safer here than she had in Midland, especially after the night before.

Chapter 3

Her dreams were of a time long ago. Courtney was an unseen visitor to the Ouendat village. She drifted gently above the scene and witnessed the life of her ancestors' people. She recognized the longhouse and knew instinctively that it was where many were gathered. The women carried wood to the longhouse. Many of the men had left the village to hunt and fish, preparing for the long winter that would come sometime soon.

She also knew instinctively that the beautiful young woman was Strong-Feather. Strong-Feather was kneeling beside some children who were playing a game that involved throwing rocks into a circle. She was young and beautiful and laughed in an innocent child-like way. She was much like Courtney had imagined she would be.

The Jesuits strolled by. She could see Strong-Feather tense as their long flowing black robes caught her line of vision. Walking along side the men of cloth was a different man. Her eyes went back down to the children and the game, but Courtney could sense Strong-Feather's tenseness around the Frenchmen. Across the village, she could see the cross that stood on top of one of the dwellings. It was their church and the men were heading towards it. Strong-Feather's eyes traveled to the backs of the men. She had a curious expression on her face. The man in the soft buckskin boots turned and looked back at her. Strong-Feather smiled softly at him, before turning and leaving the game. The man's eyes had brightened, as he caught the smile from the beautiful young woman. Courtney knew that they had exchanged a signal that meant they would meet outside of the village walls. As Strong-Feather meandered her way towards the gate of the village, she suddenly stopped. She was looking into the face of the

Ouendat medicine man.

He was much older than Strong-Feather and once again, Courtney knew instinctively that Strong-Feather had been promised by her mother to be united to an Iroquois warrior. She could sense the conflict within Strong-Feather and there was no doubt that she was afraid of the medicine man. He took Strong-Feather by the arm and pulled her forcibly towards a small bark-covered dwelling. The dwelling was where he would heal those afflicted with physical or spiritual ailments. Strong-Feather's feelings for the French traveler had been noted. The medicine man would remove the temptation from the young woman.

Strong-Feather attempted to dig in her heels to stop him from physically pulling her into the dwelling, but her attempt was in vain. The older man overpowered her and they disappeared behind the bearskin that served as the door to the dwelling. Courtney could feel the breath leave her body for the fear she felt for Strong-Feather.

In the distance, Courtney could see Strong-Feather's mother. She had promised the marriage. That was her role. Her face was weathered and devoid of expression. Courtney felt herself lift higher above the village. Strong-Feather's mother was unaware that she, too, was being watched. The Chief stood, arms folded defiantly, in front of the longhouse. He did not approve of his wife's intervention or the prospect of marriage to the brutal Iroquois nation. He did not approve, and yet as was custom, he had no jurisdiction. Courtney continued to move away from the village. Hanging outside the village was the Red Mask.

* * *

Courtney awoke from the dream with a start. A sharp pain shot from her hip. She quickly realized that her makeshift bed was completely deflated. Her hip had shoved hard into the apartment's unforgiving parquet flooring. The air mattress had obviously had a hole in it. "Oh great ... just great!" she exclaimed as she got up off of the flattened air mattress. Despite the pain, she smiled and stretched as she surveyed the empty bedroom. "My bedroom," she said. She went into the bathroom and ran the shower for the first time. Surveying herself in the mirror, she ran her fingers through her disheveled hair. As she looked around the bathroom, she smiled and exclaimed, "My bathroom!" Courtney was pleased with the apartment, even though she was still overwhelmed with the sudden change of habitat.

As she stepped into the shower, she nervously thought of the upcoming call to her parents. "Oh my God ... Jeff!" With all that had been happening, she had forgotten all about her job at the bar. Jeff would be expecting her at work that evening. She made a mental note to call him, as well, that morning.

Without warning, the warm water of the shower turned icy cold, causing Courtney to jump franticly from the tub. A flow of obscenities escaped from her mouth. She quickly grabbed a towel from the rack and wrapped herself tightly in it. "What the hell?" she exclaimed, slipping a hand back into the shower. The water had flowed warm again. She shut off the water and stepped in front of the medicine cabinet mirror. Wiping a small circle in the mirror, she saw it, but only for an instant. It was the familiar red mask. Courtney jumped back, but the image had vanished. Her heart was beating rapidly in her chest. She continued to look at the mirror that was now starting to fog again, but there was nothing. "I just imagined it," she said trying to convince herself that the image had been a figment of her imagination. The vividness of the dream returned to her. The mask had hung outside the village wall. She knew that it signified something. The mask didn't always hang there. Her mind returned to the image in the mirror. "I just imagined it!" she reiterated more forcefully.

As Courtney went to the bedroom to find something to wear, she sensed a tingling in her hands. She knew that the mask was familiar and that she had seen it other than in her dream. She tried desperately to remember where? Suddenly it dawned on her. The mask had hung in the Huronia Museum, one in a group of four masks. At one time, she had known the significance of it. She tried desperately to remember. The vividness of the dream of Strong-Feather continued to return slowly to her mind. She wondered why the mask was becoming an increasingly familiar image in her subconscious. It also seemed like it was now haunting her even in a conscious state. She feared its return.

* * *

Courtney decided to clear the image of the mask from her mind. She walked down to the small strip plaza behind the apartment building. The incident in the bathroom had shaken her, but she convinced herself that it was the stress of the last forty-eight hours that had conjured up the native images. She saw the telephone booth at the far end of the plaza. Pulling out her phone card, she dialed Jeff's home number. Jeff answered with a groggy "Hello." She had obviously woken him. "Oh my God Jeff, did I wake you?" There was a silent hesitation on the other end of the phone. "Courtney! Where the hell are you?" Courtney was now hesitant. "How did you know I'd be somewhere?" Jeff was still obviously waking up. "Uh ... Brad was by last night looking for you. He was going on and on about his stuff or something." Courtney was now silent. Jeff reiterated the question. Courtney had cleared her dry throat at the mention of Brad. "Well ... I took your advice. I'm living in the city, believe it or not." Jeff let out a surprised, "What?" Courtney laughed at the obvious shock in his voice. "I told you to go home and think about things. You sure didn't waste any time, did you?"

Courtney brought Jeff up to date about her move to the city and the night at her apartment with Brad. "He scared me, Jeff." Jeff agreed that she should be afraid. "Ya, I didn't like the side of him I saw last night either, Courtney. He said he's going to find you and get his stuff no matter what." For a moment, Courtney was silenced by the threat. "Look Jeff, I've got to go. I'm in a phone booth. I don't have a phone yet. I guess you know I won't be back to work at the bar." Jeff said he understood and told her how much he would miss her. "Look Court, call me back when you get settled and get a phone and all that." Courtney thanked him. "Oh, and Jeff, can you call Jodie and let her know what's happening? Tell her, I'll call her just as soon as I can." Jeff promised that he would. Before hanging up, he said, "Courtney. Please be careful. Brad ... well ... he was a little nuts last night." Courtney promised that she would be careful.

Courtney was feeling an awful sadness as she put the receiver back on its cradle. She liked Jeff and would miss him and the people she had worked with at 'Charlie's'. She knew, as well, that she would desperately miss having Jodie close by to confide in. She closed her eyes for a moment and then she dialed her parents' number. This was the call she didn't want to make.

"Hello?" Her mother had surprised her by answering the phone. The anxiety was clearly evident in her voice. Courtney was totally unprepared. She truly had not anticipated anyone being home. "Mom?" Mrs. Myers let out a relieved gasp. "Oh Courtney. Where have you been? We've been so worried!" Courtney could hear her father's voice in the background and then he was on the phone having obviously snatched the receiver away from Courtney's mother. "Courtney! Where the hell are you?" he yelled into the phone. Courtney desperately wanted to hang up the receiver. "I'm ... I'm in the city." She could tell that she had surprised him. "The city. What the hell are you doing there?" Her father was obviously very angry and Courtney was having difficulty preparing to give him the news, but before she could, Courtney's father continued. "Brad and his father were just here. What's this about you having some stuff of his?" Courtney didn't know quite what to say to her father. "Yes. I had some of his stuff, but I threw it all in the garbage. There was nothing of any real value in what I threw out." She could sense her father's growing anger. "Look Dad, I don't give a flying fling about Brad's stuff. Maybe it's even still in the dumpster behind the apartment, if he wants to go check. I don't know. I just called to tell you that I'm okay and tell you I'll call you when I get a phone."

Courtney hadn't dealt at all well with her father's anger. She was further unprepared for the anger that was about to explode as her father's realization that Courtney was *living* in the city hit him. "What the hell are you talking about? Now, you look here young lady. You just pack up and get back here." Courtney was struggling to contain her anger. "Look dad. I like it here. I've got an apartment and I'm not coming back right now. I want to stay here. I need to find myself." Courtney's father was deadly quiet on the other end of the phone, but Courtney recognized it as the calm before the storm. "Look, I'll call you back, dad. I have to go." Courtney hung up the phone and as the receiver hit the cradle, Courtney could hear her father's angry voice. Courtney felt guilty for having hung up the phone on him, but the conversation would only digress from there. She imagined what his next words would be. '*You, stupid Huron*' entered her mind.

* * *

As Courtney walked back to the apartment building, the tears started streaming down her face. How could she have hung up on her father? It would be perceived, as was often the case, as the ultimate show of disrespect. However, his constant criticism of her was wearing and she just couldn't stand it anymore. Courtney could never figure out why their relationship was so terribly strained. Their inability to get along went far beyond the time when she chose Hospitality and Tourism as a career. However, Doc Myers did express his great disappointment in her when she chose it over the medical field. Courtney simply didn't want to spend her life dealing with sickness and wanted a career in a field that was fun and exciting. When Courtney went to work at 'Charlie's', she knew her father was ashamed of her. He never asked her about work and she never brought up the subject. Her saving grace with her father was when it looked like she was going to marry into the local constabulary.

She wiped her tear-streaked face as she entered the building. "What am I doing?" she wondered aloud. She took the short flight of stairs up to the second floor, in an attempt to avoid Joe or any of the other tenants on the elevator. Once safely in the apartment, she cried for a long time. Courtney suddenly realized how lonely she was. Other than Jack 'the cop', and Joe 'the superintendent', she knew no one here. As Courtney stared at the plant that Jack had brought her, she remembered her reaction to the gift. She still felt terrible for having jumped to the conclusion that the presumably nice man had ulterior motives. She knew it would be a long time before she could trust another man, let alone another police officer. Courtney hesitantly went into the bathroom. She cautiously looked in the mirror but there was no red mask staring back at her. *'How silly,'* she thought. *'How absolutely ridiculous!'*

The knock at the door startled her. As she looked through the peephole, she could see Joe looking back at her. "Joe. How are you?" she said opening the door. "Come in. Please." Joe had noticed the young woman's swollen eyes. "No, no. I don't want to intrude. I was just thinking about the fact that you said you had no furniture." Courtney hadn't exactly said that, but she let Joe continue. He was looking uncomfortable about something. "Well, I hope you won't think I'm intruding or anything, but we had a tenant who left a couch. It's in storage downstairs. If you want it, it's yours until you can make arrangements." Courtney was more than touched by the offer. "Oh, that's very kind. That would be great. Thank you." Joe shuffled from one foot to the other. "Come. You see it. It's in good shape, but the colors ... well, you see. Maybe, you no want."

Joe led Courtney down to the basement of the building. It was the first time she saw where the laundry room and storage lockers were. He handed her two more keys; one for the storage room and the other for her locker. As he flicked on the lights of the room, Courtney's eyes were immediately drawn to the hideous brown and orange flowered velvet couch. She hesitated, and then said, "Wow! Yes. I see what you mean about the colors! But Joe, I'm so desperate, I'll take it." Joe was laughing as he looked at the couch. "I don't know why I keep it. I thought it was good, I guess. Here, you take the cushions and I get the dolly." Courtney attempted to carry the six cushions from the couch. They assaulted her with their musty odor. The top of the pile of cushions fell to the floor. "It looks like I'll need two trips."

Once the couch and all of the cushions were in the apartment, Courtney thanked Joe for his kindness. "It was nice of you to think of me." It appeared that Joe had taken quite a shine to the apartment's new tenant. "I think maybe someone do something bad to you, no?" Courtney was shocked by the question. "Yes, Joe. Someone did something bad to me, but it's going to be okay." Joe smiled at her. "You just let me know if you need something." Courtney did not want to overstep Joe's kindness, but asked him if she could borrow a vacuum to give the couch a good once over. "My vacuum is still at my old apartment," she explained. "Sure, sure. I get." After Joe brought her the vacuum, she went over the couch thoroughly and put the cushions out on the balcony to air out. She returned the vacuum to Joe's apartment.

After returning to her own apartment, Courtney was still thinking about Joe's kindness. A tiny knock at her door interrupted her thoughts. Looking through the peephole, she saw the top of someone's head. As she opened the door, she saw a tiny woman looking up at her. "Hello. I Maria. Joe's wife." The woman's English was quite broken and the words were somewhat hard to distinguish through her thick accent. "Joe tells me you on your own here. I brought you." Courtney looked at the large plate of what looked like perogies. "I make. Take. Try." She was smiling revealing a shiny gold filling on one of her front teeth. "This is very kind of you." Courtney couldn't believe how good the still steaming plate of food smelled. "He give you the ugly couch?" Courtney laughed. "Yes, but it beats sitting on the floor." Courtney offered for the woman to come in. "No, no. You busy. I come again. Hope you like. Joe say you nice girl." The small woman took one of Courtney's hands in hers. She looked sympathetically into Courtney's eyes. It was as if she could feel Courtney's pain. She smiled and nodded empathetically before turning and leaving.

Courtney sat at the small wicker table and enjoyed the meal that Maria had brought her. The perogies were quite delicious and Courtney certainly did appreciate the welcoming gesture. So far, the three people she had met were seemingly quite nice, although she was quite relieved that she probably wouldn't have any more dealings with Jack O'Brien. She still mistrusted his motives and the fact that he wore a uniform furthered her wish to avoid seeing him again. *They're all the same*, she thought.

Although alone, Courtney could feel a presence in the apartment. She looked up at the print above the kitchen table and it looked like the eyes of the Indian were looking down at her. She had bought it thinking it brought a familiarity to her home. The print not only hung in her mother's house, but it dawned on Courtney that she had also seen the print at the Huronia Museum across from the display of masks that had included the red mask. The museum was, ironically, a stone throw away from the Indian burial pit beside the arena. Beside the museum was a replicated Ouendat village built in the 1950's. It was built to allow visitors to the area to see what a typical village would consist of. The village stood on top of the hill that overlooked Little Lake. When Courtney was younger she had thought it had always been there. The irony of the burial pit being so close to the created village seemed unbelievable. With the discovery of the gravesite, she now wondered where the original village had been.

Her mind returned to the plate of food in front of her. She finished the delicious meal and washed the plate before returning it to Maria. She would attempt the strip plaza once more, as she wanted to grab a newspaper to look through the classified job ads and she also needed to finally pick up some groceries. Maria answered the door. "You done, so fast?" she asked excitedly. "Maria, they were absolutely delicious. Thank you, so much!" The small woman was beaming from ear to ear. "I so glad you like." Courtney was finding that she was starting to talk like Maria. "Yes. I do like. I'm going to the grocery store. Do you need anything?" Maria smiled gratefully. "No. No. We okay. You go." Maria was still smiling. She was just about the happiest person Courtney had ever met. Joe was indeed a lucky man.

Courtney returned to the plaza, her spirit elevated after Joe and Maria's extensions of kindness. She picked up some things that she needed and grabbed a newspaper on her way out of the store. Walking past the park behind the apartment building, she realized that the plastic handles of the grocery bags were starting to pinch around her hands. As she put down the bags in an effort to readjust them, she heard a familiar voice. "Hey there!" She immediately knew that it was Jack O'Brien. He had pulled up behind her in the police cruiser. "Need a ride?" Courtney wanted to decline his offer, but she didn't want to seem rude. "Sure." Courtney got in the front seat of the cruiser. "You're certainly going beyond the 'to serve' part of your motto." Jack O'Brien laughed realizing she was referring to the *'To Serve And Protect'* motto on the side of the cruiser. As they approached the building, Courtney was struggling for something to say. Should she invite him in? Jack broke the silence. "There you are, safe and sound." He got out and walked around the cruiser and opened the passenger door. "Do you need help?" Courtney was fighting every urge she had to flee into the apartment building. "No. No, I'm good. Thanks." The tall man was smiling down at her. "Good. I'll see you around." He returned to the driver side of the car, quickly got into the cruiser, and drove away. Courtney was thinking how odd the whole encounter was. He seemed to have this way of appearing right when she needed him. She wondered if it had been purely a coincidence.

Courtney struggled with the bags of groceries and let out a painful gasp when she got up to her apartment. She dropped the bags upon entering and shook her hands in an effort to get the circulation in them going again. "Next time, I'll take my car!" she exclaimed. After unloading the groceries, Courtney put some thought into her old apartment. She was unsure as to how she would manage to get the remaining things to the city. The couch that was left was really no better than the one Joe had given her, although it was a little more palatable to the eye. The bed was simply an old steel framed box spring and mattress that Brad had got somewhere. She had an inexpensive second-hand veneer clad wall unit that she wasn't all that excited about, and of course; there was the duct taped kitchen set. Still, she wanted her color television and her vacuum. Other than those two things, the superintendent could keep the rest and probably rent the apartment as 'furnished'. She would have to ask Joe if she could keep the couch a little longer. She didn't think he would have a problem with that, as there hadn't been a huge demand for it.

Courtney made herself a cup of tea and spread out the classified ads on her apartment floor. She was overwhelmed with the number of jobs that were advertised in the job market section of the paper. However, as she scoured the ads, she realized there wasn't too much listed in the hospitality section of the paper. Some of the larger hotels were advertising for kitchen staff and chefs, but Courtney knew her interest and knowledge didn't lie there. She circled the ads anyway, so that she would have the addresses of the hotels. She had wanted to start applying to the larger hotels, but she didn't have a phone for them to contact her.

Joe and Maria were most hospitable when Courtney showed up at their door a few minutes later. Joe looked up the Bell Canada service number for her, while Maria poured her a cup of tea. Bell said they would come the next day to set up the line. It would cost eighty dollars for the hook-up. After a short visit with her new friends, she returned to her apartment. Courtney was disheartened by the expense, but she knew there was nothing she could do, as she needed a phone. She would have to wait to go downtown until after she had a phone number to put on her job applications.

* * *

THE RED MASK

Just after ten the next morning, the service technician from the phone company arrived. He ran through the phone costs with Courtney and told her they would be reflected on her first telephone bill. She was happy she could defer the payment for a month. After the technician left, she scoured the two huge telephone books he had left. She added to her list of larger hotels. She would have to stop by a bookstore and buy a guidebook to Toronto. She would need to learn more about the city, if she planned to work in the hospitality industry. She decided that now was as good a time as any to venture out and begin her search for a job.

* * *

The bus arrived in front of the apartment building and Courtney desperately searched through her wallet for the required change posted on the ticket box. The bus jolted to a start and Courtney swung around nearly landing in the lap of an elderly woman seated in the handicapped and elderly seat behind the driver. Courtney apologized to the lady who didn't even seem to notice what had just about happened. She was tempted to shoot the driver a nasty look believing that he had found some pleasure in doing this, but his gaze was clearly focused on the road in front of the bus. His right hand extended a transfer to her for the subway connection. Courtney thought that the hand looked mechanical, lacking any connection to the driver.

As the bus meandered through the surrounding neighborhood, Courtney had a good opportunity to see the section of the city that she had now made her home. Large maple and oak trees lined the streets, their leaves creating a soft canopy over the neighborhood. Thick black wires crossed overhead like a protective checkerboard above the city streets. Once at the station, the bus let out an exhaustive gasp as the doors swung open. When she started towards the station entrance, she was overwhelmed with the bustle of activity. She wondered what it would possibly be like by the end of the day. She handed her transfer to the transit worker at the booth and stood confused in front of two possible staircases. She remembered the outstretched map on the hood of her car and realized that she wanted to go east. Returning to the booth, she attempted to get the attention of the transit worker. "Excuse me ... EXCUSE ME!" People, coming through the turnstiles, nastily jostled her. "Do you have any subway maps?" The man simply slipped a map through the small opening in the same mechanical way the driver had handed her the transfer. His gaze did not leave the ticket box. "Thanks!" Courtney was unsure if he had heard her extension of gratitude.

As she stood on the eastbound platform, she made sure to stand well back of the yellow line, as indicated by the many signs stating that you should do so. Her fellow passengers seemed oblivious to the signs as they stood well over the line, their bodies dangerously close to where the train would be when it would pull in. When it finally did arrive, it sent a gust of musty tunnel air into the station. Courtney watched as people scurried in every direction to secure a seat. It reminded her of a huge game of musical chairs. A large man sat in the seat next to her. His leg brushed against hers. He seemed oblivious to how close he was to her. Courtney felt that her personal space was being invaded. It felt terribly uncomfortable and unfamiliar. She longed to escape the touch of the stranger. Courtney was relieved when the man got off the train three stops later.

It took only twenty minutes to arrive at Yonge and Bloor, which she had always understood to be the hub of the city. As she exited the station into an underground shopping concourse, she was greeted by an incredible amount of activity. Well-dressed people hustled by her, intent on reaching their destinations. She felt invisible, as she stood in wonder and watched. Exiting to the outside world, she looked up at the vast array of towers and saw some large hotels in the distance. She was so busy looking up that she didn't notice the panhandler that was seated against the base of a building, his hand lazily outstretched. Courtney nearly tripped over him, but caught sight of him at the last minute. It was obvious to her that he was native and her heart beat rapidly at the sight of him. Panhandlers were not a part of her other world, and it broke her heart to see the desperation of the native person.

Courtney entered the posh lobby of the Park Plaza Hotel, which was the first hotel she happened upon. The opulence of the hotel was in striking contrast to the panhandler she had seen moments before. The concierge was located in the center of the lobby and Courtney decided she would ask him for directions to the Human Resource

Department of the hotel. The elderly sharply dressed man, attired in a burgundy, gold-tasseled uniform, directed her to the Personnel Department located through the back of the hotel. Before going there, she toured the main floor of the hotel overwhelmed by the décor of the meeting rooms, the classy restaurants and the cozy pub. Her heart beat in excitement. The hotel was stunning. There was certainly nothing even remotely comparable in Midland.

Once in the Personnel Department, Courtney went to the counter and waited for the secretary to finish inputting something into the computer. She looked up at Courtney and continued to type. After several minutes, she came to the counter. "Yes?" she queried rudely. "Yes. Hello. I'm looking for a job. May I have an application?" The woman quickly surveyed Courtney up and down. She slipped her hand under the counter and put an application form on top. "Just leave the parts out that are already on your resume." Courtney felt a little silly. "I ... I don't have a resume." The woman seemed annoyed and rolled her eyes skyward. "Oh," she huffed. The woman returned to her desk and continued typing. As the woman hadn't offered her one, Courtney rummaged through her purse for a pen. After completing the application, Courtney returned to the counter. "Just leave it there. We'll let you know." The woman didn't even look at her. Courtney repeated this procedure at the half a dozen hotels she visited that afternoon.

Exhausted and frustrated, she decided she just wanted to go back to the apartment and soak her sore feet and body in a hot bath. The adventure into the city was a bit overwhelming and Courtney slinked into the tub. The hot water surrounded her and helped alleviate the stress that had built up in her neck. She closed her eyes and relived the events of the day. The face of the Indian panhandler entered her thoughts. It had saddened her to see the man, so obviously destitute. Many natives lived this life of impoverishment and she knew that hope was non-existent for so many. Her thoughts of the native man were interrupted when she heard a distant knock at the door. She listened intently and then she heard the knock again. Courtney debated whether she should get out of the tub or not? She wanted to remain in the tranquility of the tub, but the knock continued. "Damn it!" She quickly jumped out of the tub, dried herself off, and dressed in her sweats. As she looked through the peephole to see who it was, she suddenly jumped away from the door. Grasping her chest that housed her rapidly beating heart, she stood frozen as the knocking continued. She slowly inched back towards the door and looked through the peephole again. The red mask had been replaced by the image of Jack O'Brien. She opened the door cautiously.

* * *

"You look like you've seen a ghost!" Courtney realized that she must have looked frightened standing in front of him. Her heart was still beating rapidly in her chest. "I ... I guess I thought I had." Jack O'Brien was still looking curiously at her. "I'm okay. Come in." Just then the phone started ringing startling Courtney further. "Hang on," she said laughing nervously at her sudden popularity. She had listed her phone number on the application forms and couldn't believe that there was already a call. "Hello," she said anxiously. "How long did you think it would take me to find you?" The voice on the other end of the phone was Brad's. Courtney stood in shocked silence. She quickly hung up the phone. "Hey, you got a phone?" Jack said. "Who was that?" Courtney lied. "I don't know. The line was dead." Courtney quickly bent to unplug the phone. "Maybe you can help me? I don't know if it should go in the kitchen or in here?" Courtney made her way to the living room. "Isn't it amazing that a one bedroom apartment has two phone jacks?" Courtney's heart was still racing. She had put the phone down, but hadn't plugged it back in. "Hey what do you think of my couch? Pretty ugly, eh?"

Jack noticed Courtney's nervousness, but knew, for whatever reason; she didn't want him to know who was really on the phone. "Holy cow!" he pretended to play along. "Nice. You didn't pay money for that did you?" Courtney told him the story of how Joe had moved the couch up from the basement the day before. "Aren't you going to plug the phone back in?" he asked mostly to see her reaction. "Oh. Yes. Why yes. I am." Courtney hesitated. "Once I figure out where it should go." Jack had a concerned expression on his face. "Courtney. I know you hardly know me, but maybe you should tell me who was really on the phone. Maybe I can help." Courtney looked up at the tall stranger, her eyes filling with tears. "Jack, it's a really long story." Jack smiled gently at her. The laugh lines on his face were visible. "I've got some time." He proceeded to park himself on the couch.

"Actually," Courtney said, "Would you mind if we go for a walk?" His smile was so tender. Courtney felt like blurting out the whole awful story of Brad right away, but she left the room to brush her still wet hair and throw on some more appropriate clothes for her walk with him. Walking out of the building in silence, Courtney finally took a deep breath before starting her story. "I was engaged to be married and the wedding was to take place last weekend." Jack asked her if she had a change of heart. "No, not me. Him! He called it off a few weeks ago." Jack empathized that it must have hurt her deeply. "Oh, I was pretty devastated all right. I guess I still am." Jack continued. "Ah, hence the move to the big city?" Courtney stopped walking and looked deeply into the eyes of the handsome man. "Well, not quite." Courtney filled him in on all of the details. She told him about the lie about her wanting to have a relationship with Brad's partner. "Brad is a cop, too." Jack nodded. "I see. Now some of it is making sense." Courtney wasn't entirely sure what he meant.

The pair continued to walk along until Courtney broke the silence, mostly in an effort to be polite. "So, now that I've opened up to you about all of the dirt in my life, how about you tell me something about your life?" Jack chuckled. "Okay, but it's really pretty boring." Courtney laughed, as well. "Hey, I grew up in Midland. It doesn't get any more boring than that." Jack smiled. "I'm sure that's not true." Jack took a deep breath before continuing. "I did grow up, like you did, in a small community. Mine was on the outskirts of Niagara on the Lake. My family was originally from Quebec, but my grandparents on my mother's side moved to Niagara in the early 1920's." Courtney was surprised that Jack's family was originally from Quebec. She had visited the quaint town of Niagara on the Lake and she remembered it for its homes with brightly colored gingerbread trim. "My parents own a vineyard. They grow grapes for a local winery." Courtney said she thought that was pretty neat. "Yes. It was a pretty neat life, I guess. Two of my brothers still work there." Courtney had no siblings and asked Jack how many he had. "Five. Five brothers." Courtney couldn't believe it. "Oh, your poor mother. Any sisters?" Jack laughed. "No! But I have five sister-in laws, so the pressure is on for me to complete the O'Brien family."

Courtney was starting to warm up to Jack. *He does seem nice*, she thought. "So, what's taking you so long? What about this girl of yours?" Courtney gently nudged him. "Well, actually, we haven't known each other that long. It's kind of hard to say right now." Courtney was curious about the woman in Jack's life. "So, what's she like?" Jack smiled. "Well, she's very pretty. She has a warm personality, and well ... we'll see." Jack's voice was trailing a bit. Courtney was a little surprised that she could feel a bit of a knot in her stomach. She had an inexplicable feeling of jealousy towards the woman that had obviously worked her way into this man's life. She hoped that she could some day find someone she could trust and allow into her life again. For now, she knew it would be a long time before she would be able to trust again.

"Hey, I have an idea." Jack broke Courtney's thoughts. "There's a nice little Italian restaurant a couple of blocks from here and I'm starving. You want to grab a bite to help take your mind off of your troubles?" Courtney thanked Jack, but said she had left her wallet and purse back at the apartment. "That's okay. You can pay me back later." Jack sped up, apparently not taking no for an answer. "Jack, aren't you forgetting something?" For a second, Jack looked surprised. "Brad?" Courtney laughed. "No, he can wait, but what would your girlfriend think about you having dinner with another woman?" Jack was looking pensive for a moment. "Well, she's a pretty secure person. I'm sure it wouldn't be an issue, if I explained the circumstances." Courtney laughed. "Well, she must be pretty secure. If my boyfriend told me he met a woman in a park, found her an apartment, bought her a plant, and took her to dinner all in forty-eight hours, I don't think I'd be as secure about the circumstances!" Jack smiled. "Yes. I guess you're right. On the other hand, if she still understands, then maybe she IS the one!" Courtney said it under her breath, "Yes ... or very foolish." Jack had heard the comment but kept on walking.

* * *

Jack stopped in front of the small Italian eatery. Courtney would have walked right on by, if he hadn't stopped her by gently taking her arm. "Here." Courtney looked at the front of the restaurant.

"Gees. I didn't even see it. How ever did you find it?" Jack said he was pretty aware of what was in the neighborhood. Courtney realized that of course he would be, being stationed in the area.

As they entered through the front door, Courtney looked around at the small intimate restaurant. "Jacky!" A small Italian woman was running up to them. The woman was looking so pleased to see Jack that Courtney felt immediately comfortable in the setting. "Paula, this is my good friend, Courtney." The woman took Courtney's hand in hers and started shaking it profusely. "Hello ... hello. I get you a nice table by the window." As Paula started to head towards the front of the restaurant, Jack caught up and stopped her. "Actually, Paula, do you have anything further back?" The woman said that she did. Courtney wondered if Jack didn't want the window seat for fear of being spotted. Maybe his girlfriend wasn't that secure after all?

Once settled in a secluded booth in the back of the restaurant, Jack asked, "What's good today, Paula?" The little woman laughed. "Oh Jacky, you know everything here is good! But you're in luck today. Joseph made some homemade tortellini that is just out of this world." It was Jack's turn to laugh, as Paula had kissed her pinched thumb and fingers in a descriptive gesture. "Sounds good, Paula. How about you Courtney, would you like a menu?" Courtney agreed that Paula was the expert and ordered the tortellini. The little woman smiled at Courtney. "You won't be sorry. You need some wine?" Courtney said that a glass of red wine would be lovely. Jack settled the order. "Bring us a half-liter of Shiraz, please Paula."

Paula arrived back promptly and poured two glasses of the deep red wine. Jack began by opening up more about his life with his five brothers. Courtney couldn't believe how at ease she was starting to feel with him. The strong Italian wine was also having an illicit affect on her and she could feel her stress about Brad's call start to dissipate. As Jack talked on, she was not only enjoying his stories, but she was starting to think more about the fact that he was indeed strikingly handsome. His warm dimpled smile and deep blue eyes were beginning to draw her in. Suddenly, Courtney asked, "So what's your girlfriend's name?" Jack was surprised by the question, as he was in the middle of a story about his brother, Carl. He smiled, looking at Courtney's empty wine glass. "Ellen. Her name is Ellen."

"More wine?" he asked teasingly. "Good idea!" As Paula came

back to the table with the steaming plates of tortellini, Jack ordered another half-liter of wine. Paula said, "Now you be careful, Courtney. You don't want him taking advantage of you." Jack smiled impishly at Paula. "Paula, now you know I'm not the type of man who would take advantage of a woman who's been drinking." Paula gave him a look and wagged her index finger at him. "Well, you'd better not, or you'll have me to deal with!" Jack's laugh was rich and deep.

"Why the sudden interest in my girlfriend, Courtney? You're not becoming smitten with me are you?" he asked teasingly. "Me, with you? Hell no! I've been down the cop road, thank you very much!" If Jack was disappointed by her words, he didn't show it. He simply let out a huge laugh. "Well, we're not all bad. Do you think that a different line of work would have changed your Brad into a decent guy?" Courtney was trying hard to think about what Jack had just said. "Maybe not? I don't know?" Jack told her not to close any doors on herself just because of a man's line of work. Courtney retaliated. "Well, haven't you ever heard the saying 'Once bitten, twice shy'?" Jack retorted with, "Well, haven't you every heard the saying 'Thee who hesitates is lost'." The banter continued when Courtney responded with "Look before you leap!" They both started to laugh.

Paula returned to the table with the wine. "You are such a nice couple. You keep her Jack! You be good to her!" Paula's words seemed to have a sobering affect on Courtney. "Paula, I don't think his girlfriend would like that!" Paula looked sternly at Jack. "Oh, Jacky?" Jack leaned back in his chair and folded his arms across his chest. Paula wagged her right index finger at Jack again, before leaving the table.

"So tell me about your Indian roots. I find that part of you extremely intriguing." Courtney looked soberly at her dinner companion. "Well, I'll give you the abridged version." Courtney filled Jack in on her mother's great-great-great grandmother and the French explorer she had run away with. "Didn't they find an Ouendat burial pit in Midland a little while ago?" Courtney was surprised that Jack knew of the discovery and was pleased that he now used the term 'Ouendat'. "I read about it in the Toronto Star. They are still trying to figure out what to do about it, aren't they?" Courtney knew that the Ouendat believed that when their people died, they had two souls; one that stayed with the body and one that moved on to the after-life. The fact that the site had been disturbed would mean that the souls had been disturbed. "Yes. I'm sure the elders are very upset that the site has been disturbed." Courtney thought of the masked face that had been haunting her. She wondered if she should tell Jack about it. She decided to avoid the topic, as he would probably think she was crazy. Courtney changed the subject back to the vineyard.

After dinner, Jack talked Courtney into trying a cappuccino. Courtney somehow doubted she would ever get to sleep that night after the strong rich coffee. Jack settled up the bill with Paula and they started to walk back to Courtney's apartment. Courtney still felt a little light-headed after the strong Italian wine. When Jack linked an arm through hers, she made no protestation.

Walking arm in arm, Courtney told Jack about her father and mother. Jack was surprised that Courtney's father was a doctor. "Always good to have one in the family. Do you have any brothers or sisters?" She told him she didn't. "How did your parents really handle your move to the city? It must be hard on them losing their only child to the wiles of city life?" She remembered the conversation she had with them the day before. She didn't answer the question. "You've told them?" Courtney simply responded that she had. As they approached the building, they didn't notice the pick-up at the far end of the parking area on the side of the building. Brad was looking in his rear view mirror. "Tramp!" he said hitting his hand hard on the steering wheel of the truck.

As Courtney and Jack approached the front of the building, Jack surprised Courtney by saying, "Well, I guess I should go." Courtney insisted that she needed to give him some money for dinner. "Besides Jack, I would appreciate your support while I call Brad. Would you mind? Please?" Jack seemed touched by her obvious need of his support. "Sure. Okay. But only if you let me pay for dinner." Courtney didn't want to agree, but finally gave in. She felt like she didn't want the evening to end. She had to admit that she had enjoyed his company. He had taken away some of her loneliness.

Once in the apartment, Courtney dialed the number of the Laduke house. Jack stayed in the kitchen, affording her some privacy. "Mr. Laduke. It's Courtney Myers. Is Brad there? ... No. Well, do you know when he'll be in? ... "Yes. Well I know. I've moved. Look, I'm sorry the way that worked out, but I don't have Brad's things. I threw them out when he called off the marriage! ... Compensation? Look, Mr. Laduke, I don't want to be rude, but who's going to compensate me for the wedding dress?" Jack could hear the conversation. He was thinking that she had spirit, but knew that it was very difficult for her. "Well, that's bologna! He did a pretty good job on my reputation with his lies. That's right! Your son is a big fat liar!" Removing the phone from her ear, she said, "He hung up on me." Jack laughed. "Apparently!"

Suddenly there was a pounding at the door. Courtney looked through the peephole. "Oh my God! It's him! It's Brad! Jesus, what should I do?" Courtney could see that Jack had tensed. "Well, he doesn't waste any time, does he?" Jack surprised Courtney by brushing by her and opening the door. The larger man standing in front of Brad had obviously surprised him. "Hey pal, this is between me and her!" Brad was pointing an accusatory finger at Courtney. "I don't think so ... pal! I know all about you. Now why don't you just settle down and tell me what you want with her?" Courtney was silent, somewhat enjoying seeing Brad squirm in front of the larger man. "She knows damn well what I want. She's got some stuff of mine. Now, why don't you just butt out?"

Courtney jumped in. "I threw it all out, Brad." Brad's anger was growing. "That's illegal, Courtney." Courtney, voice quivering, retaliated. "Yes. Well so is slander Brad and I'd say you did a fairly good job to my reputation." Brad was undaunted. "What a joke! It wasn't me that was messing around! You wrecked your own reputation, my dear!" Courtney removed the engagement ring from her finger and shaking gave it to Brad. Jack jumped in. "Okay buddy, you got what you came for. Just accept that your other stuff is gone!" Brad turned his attention on Jack. "Maybe you don't know who you are dealing with?" Brad reached in his pocket and brought out his badge. "Ya, well right back at you pal!" Jack had reciprocated by bringing out his badge. Brad stood with a look of surprise on his face. "What's this Courtney? Isn't this your third cop in two months? Cops have a name for girls like you." Brad turned hard on his heel and stormed away down the hall.

Jack and Courtney stood in a brief moment of silence. They then turned and looked at each other. "Oh, thank you Jack! I don't know what I would have done if you weren't here!" Courtney ran impulsively into his arms and began to cry. "It's okay. It's going to be okay." Jack held her close and gently ran a hand down her long sleek hair. Courtney was breathing in the sweet scent of his cologne. After a moment, Jack lifted Courtney's tear-streaked face up to his. "It's okay. He's gone." Courtney smiled and then started to laugh softly. "Did you see his face when you brought out your badge?" Jack laughed, too. "Yes. I sure did!" Jack continued to hold her. She could feel the sudden tenseness pass through his body as he broke the embrace.

"Look, I'd better get going ... unless you *want* me to stay? I don't think that guy will be back tonight." Jack was glancing uncomfortably at his watch. "Oh my God. I'm so sorry Jack. I've probably kept you from your girlfriend. I'm so sorry." Jack smiled. "It's okay. You haven't interfered at all. Listen, how about if you take my number? I'm not far away and could be here in a couple of minutes, if you need me." Courtney began the search for a piece of paper and a pen. "Yes. It's nice to know there is someone who I can call. Thanks!" Jack asked Courtney to do him a favor. "Call your parents, Courtney. I think it would be wise to mend that fence." Courtney knew it would be difficult, but nodded her head in agreement. "Good girl. Oh, and bolt your door. Just in case."

After Jack left, Courtney sat alone in her apartment. She was somehow aware that Jack was sitting in his car in the parking lot. He stayed there for over two hours. He had wanted her, but knew the timing was wrong. He hadn't liked the guy that had come to her door. Jack knew he was trouble.

Courtney put on some comfortable pajamas and slipped into her sleeping bag on the couch. As she closed her eyes a small smile crept across her face. She thought the words. *Okay, I like him. Too bad he's taken. Actually, thank God he's taken. There will be no more cops in my life.* Courtney was absolutely determined that she wouldn't fall for Jack. As she replayed the events of the day over in her mind, she felt her mind drifting back to the look on Brad's face when Jack brought out his badge. She also thought about the embrace. She couldn't help but relive the feeling of security she had felt being held by him. It had felt so right having his strong arms wrapped around her. She thought of his girlfriend and was riddled with conflicting emotion. As right as it had felt for the moment, it was wrong on many levels. She wanted her dreams to deal with the strange emotions she was feeling, but sleep eluded her for most of the night.

When sleep did eventually come, Courtney found herself back in the Ouendat village. Days had passed since Strong-Feather had been taken behind the bearskin door. She saw Strong-Feather's mother enter the dwelling with food for her daughter. Courtney waited for her to exit. Eventually, Strong-Feather came from the dwelling assisted by her mother. Her face lacked the child-like quality she had when Courtney had seen her last. Her eyes were haunting. Dark circles enveloped them. Courtney wondered what torture she had endured. Her question was answered. Strong-Feather looked blindly towards the sun. Courtney knew her sight had been taken. She would be unable to look into his eyes again, to see the love he felt for her. They had punished her for her indiscretion. Courtney could see him. Falling to his knees, he covered his face with his hands. He knew what had happened. He vowed to take her away.

Chapter 4

The sun was beaming through the sliding doors of the balcony, illuminating the living room. Courtney struggled to focus on the brightness of the room, but her eyes closed wearily and all she could see was a familiar red canvass. As her eyes fought to accept the morning light, she began to think about all that had happened to her since her move to the city.

Courtney's mind traveled back to the way she had run into Jack's arms the night before. She now felt a little silly about her need to be held by him. She wrote it off to the combination of the fear of Brad and, to a lesser extent, the wine that she had consumed at the restaurant. There was no denying that Jack had made her feel safe. The sweet smell of his cologne had enveloped her. She closed her eyes to the memory. "This is ridiculous!" she cried as she got up off the couch. Standing too quickly, the annoying pain returned to the back of her head. Her vision blurred. Courtney lay back down to try and alleviate the throbbing pain.

Eventually the pain did begin to subside. Courtney decided she wouldn't go back downtown until the next day. Rifling through a box of sheets she had brought from the old apartment, she exclaimed, "Okay, these will have to do for now." Courtney found her small sewing kit and pulled out a needle and a spool of white thread. Her challenge would be to come up with some sort of inexpensive rod for the curtains that would hang over the sliding balcony doors. She remembered seeing, on one of those home-decorating shows, that copper plumbing pipe worked in a pinch.

Courtney figured there were two types of mornings. They were either tea mornings or the tougher, more necessary, coffee mornings.

After a cup of coffee, she would have to find a hardware store and buy the two three-and-a-half foot pieces of pipe and the brackets she would need for the curtain rod.

She found Joe sweeping the front walkway to the building. He looked happy to see his new tenant and gave her directions to the closest hardware store. She bought an extra piece of pipe for the bottom of the sliding doors, so that they couldn't be opened from the outside. On her way home, she saw a small fabric store and decided to stop and buy some wide ribbon for the ties. She selected a dark brown ribbon that would at least tie in with the deep orange and brown colors of the couch. She was becoming increasingly excited about the project. It would afford her some much-needed privacy and a bit of added security.

* * *

After an afternoon of sewing, Courtney stood back and surveyed her handiwork. She had worked diligently on the curtains and was proud of how nice they had turned out. When six o'clock arrived, Courtney remembered her promise to Jack to call her mom and dad. She picked up the handset of her new telephone and dialed her parents' number. "Mom. Hi, it's me." Her mother was relieved to hear her daughter's voice. She asked her mother if her father was there. "He's still at the office, dear. Are you okay? Where are you?" Courtney told her mom about her new apartment and how happy she was with it. She told her mom about Joe and Maria. "Mom, I'm very excited about this. I know you and dad may not approve, but I really needed to do this." Eve Myers told her daughter it wasn't that they didn't approve. "It was all just so sudden. It really took us by surprise, honey."

Courtney filled her mother in about Brad. "Are you okay? Did he hurt you?" She reassured her mother that she was okay. "I had a friend here. His name is Jack." It felt funny to refer to Jack as a friend. She really only barely knew him. Courtney's mother teasingly asked, "Jack is it? Where did he come from?" Courtney assured her mother that he was just a friend. "Besides, he's otherwise engaged, so to speak." Her mother was silent for a few seconds. "So, by otherwise engaged ... do you mean, well ... gay? I know there are a lot of them in the city." Courtney laughed hysterically. "No, mom. He's certainly not gay. Trust me! Look mom, here's my phone number. I can't talk long because of the charges." Courtney could hear her mother fumbling around for a pen. She eventually found one and took down Courtney's telephone number. "Mom, I love you." Her mother told her she loved her too and made Courtney promise to be careful. "I'll call you back in a few days and let you know what's happening with my job search." As Courtney hung up the phone, she thought how ironic that the only danger she had experienced in the city, so far, had been from Brad.

Once again, her thoughts were drifting back to the night before. It troubled her that it wasn't so much the incident with Brad that occupied her, but the embrace with Jack. She imagined what could have happened. Their lips were touching. He was kissing her softly at first and then the kiss deepened. "Jesus!" She reprimanded herself for such foolish thoughts.

She didn't think it was strange that the telephone was ringing. She, somehow, knew instinctively that it was Jack. She answered with a hint of seduction in her voice. At first Jack was silent, obviously caught off guard. "Courtney?" he asked confused by the seduction. "Hi," she said the seduction still evident in her voice. "Sorry. I didn't recognize your voice." She laughed softly. "I just, uh … called to make sure you're okay?" Courtney was catapulted back to reality and she, once again, felt foolish about her thoughts. "I'm fine Jack." It was a simple conversation, but it was riddled with strange emotion. Courtney's voice was warm and friendly, but the initial seductiveness had confused him. "Good. Well … I was just concerned. I'm glad you're okay." Courtney felt powerless. The seductive tone returned to her voice. "I'm fine. Really fine, Jack." She hung up the phone softly. Snapping back to reality, she asked herself, "*What am I doing? Silly girl!*" She laughed remembering the conversation with her mother. "For Pete's sakes, he's gay!" She thought that if she could only keep that image in her mind, she wouldn't be tempted to cross the line with him again. Once more, she laughed at the impossibility of Jack's sexual preference being anything but heterosexual.

* * *

The memories of her dreams the next morning were devoid of the Ouendat village. Courtney had awoken refreshed and, once again, stood proudly looking at her handiwork from the previous day. Her thoughts drifted to Jodie, and she decided to call her friend to tell her about her new apartment. Courtney was disappointed when there was no answer at her best friend's apartment. If Jeff had called Jodie, then Courtney knew that Jodie would be upset that Courtney hadn't called her yet. Her watch read 'seven-thirty'. She knew it was pointless to call Jodie at work, as she didn't start until nine o'clock. She would try to call later on that day.

Courtney ventured back into the heart of the city and applied at some of the larger hotels in the southern section of the downtown. She was overwhelmed by the grandeur and size of the hotels she visited. As she entered the Personnel Department of the Royal York Hotel, one of the oldest and most opulent hotels in the city, she was now becoming used to the procedure of dealing with personnel departments.

A sharply dressed silver-haired man was standing outside one of the offices in the department. Courtney couldn't help but overhear the conversation between him and the female voice inside of the office. "For Pete's sake Diane, just phone a temp agency. It's straight typing of purchase orders. How hard can it be to get someone to do that?" The woman inside the office said that she would see what she could do. The man angrily responded that her attempts just weren't good enough. "Look Diane, I needed someone yesterday! You should see the mess on the desk! I simply can't wait another day!"

As the man turned to walk past Courtney, Courtney stopped him. Her heart was beating furiously in excitement. "Excuse me? Did I hear you say you are looking for a typist?" The man hesitated and looked at the pretty young woman in front of him. "Do you type?" he asked abruptly. Courtney had taken a typing course at college and had been, at one time, fairly proficient on a keyboard. "Yes. I can type." He looked skyward as if to thank the typing Gods. He then returned to the woman's office and closed the door. A minute later the red-faced woman opened the office door and came over to Courtney.

"I'm Diane Clark. We're looking for a typist for our purchasing department. It's a temporary position for six months due to a maternity leave. Would you be interested ... in applying?" The woman had spoken loud enough for the man to hear. Courtney's hands were sweating. This was truly the break she needed. The woman continued. "Well, I'll need you to fill out an application and do a typing test." Courtney said she would be glad to, although she worried about how she would do on a typing test. It had been a while since she had typed, and she could feel the nervous sweat on her palms.

After completing the application and doing the test, Courtney was ushered into the personnel recruiter's office. The older man was sitting in one of the office chairs. Diane Clark indicated to Courtney that she should sit in the chair beside the gentleman. "Courtney, this is Robert Small. Mr. Small has an immediate need for a typist. You did fairly well on your typing test ... 55 words per minute, but I notice you have very limited work experience." Courtney agreed. "Yes. But if I don't prove up to your satisfaction, you can simply let me go." Diane Clark seemed a little surprised by the young woman's assertive response. Robert Small was smiling from ear to ear. "Okay Diane. I like her. Can you start now?" Courtney also knew she liked Robert Small. Diane Clark, feeling powerless, was taken aback by the whole situation. "Robert, I need to reference check." Robert Small responded. "Well, do you reference check the temps that we get through those agencies you deal with?" Diane Clark said that she didn't, but Courtney would be on the hotel's payroll. "There's a difference, Robert." Mr. Small was obviously frustrated with procedure. "Diane, I will take responsibility for her if she doesn't pan out. Where do you want me to sign?"

The recruiter knew that she was beat. "Well, we haven't even discussed a wage." Robert Small asked her how much she paid her temps through the agency. "Well, fifteen, but we get a guarantee!" Mr. Small was obviously well aware of temporary agencies. "Yes, and if you make them permanent, you pay exorbitant fees. Courtney won't cost us a red cent if it all works out. Fifteen it is!" As Robert Small got up, Diane Clark stood as well. "Come on Courtney!" Diane Clark was obviously embarrassed by the way she had been treated. "Robert, there is paperwork that I need her to fill out." Her voice had trailed into an almost whisper. "Tell you what, Diane. You fill out what you can, and when you're ready for Courtney, bring the paperwork on up." Courtney could sense that Diane Clark was totally exasperated. She was a recruiter and was used to wielding a certain power that went along with the position. "Come on Courtney," Robert Small reiterated. Diane Clark drew in a breath. "Yes. Go. I'll be by in an hour or so." As Courtney walked to the elevator with her new boss, she now knew, for certain, that she truly liked him. He had got her a job in a matter of minutes at a rate that exceeded her expectations. "Thank you, sir." He glanced over at her. "Robert ... please! Oh, and you're certainly welcome."

* * *

As Courtney and Mr. Small took the short elevator ride up to the second floor, he briefed Courtney on the position. "The hours are nine to five, Monday to Friday. You'll have one hour for lunch, which I would prefer you took from noon until one. The job isn't terribly exciting. It's straight data input into the computer. We have six purchasing agents that purchase everything from sheets to silverware for our hotels. The purchasing agent writes out the purchase order, and then they give it to you for input. Pretty simple stuff really." He paused, as they stepped from the elevator. "Our secretary left on maternity leave three weeks ago. We have a backlog of work on the desk. I don't understand why a personnel department takes so; pardon the expression, *damn* long to get a temp? I'm sorry for the mess you're walking into. Anita, one of our purchasing agents, will show you what you have to do. You'll be on your own tomorrow. Any questions?" Courtney was a little overwhelmed by the amount of information the man had just given her. "No. I think I have it all." Mr. Small smiled at her. "Good girl!"

As Courtney was led into the purchasing department, she was overwhelmed by the opulence of the surroundings. In the middle of the department was a small pond. Courtney saw koi swimming lazily in the water. The soothing sound of the water was in contrast to the nervousness that Courtney felt inside, but she knew that she was going to like the soft trickling resonance.

Robert Small entered one of the back cubicles in the department. A beautiful sharply dressed woman looked up from behind a desk. "Anita. This is Courtney Myers. She's our new typist." The woman, who was not much older than Courtney, smiled. "Oh, thank God!" she said. Robert Small asked the woman if she would mind showing Courtney the ropes. "Not at all. Anything to get those damn purchase orders done!" Once again, the woman looked skyward thanking God for Courtney's arrival. Courtney chuckled at the now familiar gesture.

Anita led Courtney to the desk beside one of the department's large windows that looked out at the train station across Front Street. She spoke enthusiastically. "I'm so happy you're here. It's pretty simple really. I'll show you the computer program and get you started." Courtney watched the young woman turn on the computer. She entered a password that she whispered to Courtney. "Union." It was the name of the train station that Courtney had viewed from the window. Anita called up a blank purchase order and then led Courtney through a couple of examples. Courtney couldn't believe that she was going to make fifteen dollars an hour for this. "A couple of times a day, you'll need to print them and the purchasing agent signs them. Then they go to Robert for his approval. They are kept in Robert's office in binders and are filed by hotel and then by date of purchase. Come on, I'll show you where the binders are." Anita and Courtney went into Mr. Smalls' office. Courtney was overwhelmed by the beautiful décor of the surroundings. Richly decorated in deep mahogany, she dreamt secretly that she would some day be afforded such a lush office of her own. She vowed that she would work hard to try and achieve the reward that years of dedication obviously provided in the hospitality industry.

After showing Courtney the binders, Anita looked down at her watch. "Hey. It's lunchtime. Would you like to join me?" Courtney explained that she was a bit anxious to get started on the huge amount of orders on the desk. "How about tomorrow Anita? I'd love to have lunch with you then." Anita smiled. "Hey, remember that enthusiasm a month from now when you're sick to death of purchase orders. I understand, though. We're all keeners when we start. Tomorrow would be fine." Before leaving, Anita turned to her new co-worker. "Courtney, welcome aboard. We're glad you're here." Courtney had a good feeling about her new job.

* * *

Diane Clark appeared shortly after the purchasing agents had returned from lunch. She brought a crisp, new personnel file with her that housed some paperwork that Courtney would have to fill out. Courtney could tell that the older woman was still perturbed by the lack of procedure that had led to Courtney's employment with the Royal York. Her demeanor was curt, bordering on rude. "Paydays are every second Friday. You'll get a check next Friday. We can auto deposit your pay with the CIBC downstairs. If you give me a void check by tomorrow, we can do it by next Friday. Otherwise, we'll just cut you a check." Courtney's enthusiasm was unaffected by the woman's manner. "I'll probably open an account." For some reason the woman seemed further perturbed. "You'll be paid for a full day today, even though you didn't start until eleven." Courtney was initially unsure whether she should thank the woman for the full days' pay. She had, after all, worked through her lunch. She decided to thank her anyway.

Throughout the day, each of the purchasing agents made their way down to Courtney's desk to introduce themselves. Her initial impression of all of them was quite positive. She got the feeling from them that the previous secretary wasn't all that thrilled with the job. They seemed relieved to have Courtney in the position. Robert Small came back from lunch and stopped by to see how Courtney was making out. "Good, Mr. Small. I'll leave what I've completed on your desk by three." Robert Small smiled. "If you call me Mr. Small again, I'll have to fire you. It's Robert." Courtney laughed. "Yes ... Robert! I don't want to get fired on my first day." Her new boss walked away, wearing a broad smile.

Courtney created individual signing files for each of the purchasing agents. She left the files with the agents vowing to come back in an hour to pick them up. Everyone was impressed with Courtney's efficiency, but none more than Robert Small. He had shown Diane Clark a thing or two about hiring, and that had made his day. Courtney arrived in his office at exactly three o'clock with fifty purchase orders for him to approve. As he flipped through his 'to sign' file that Courtney had made for him, he was now beaming. "Okay. Just tell me you're coming back tomorrow?" Courtney laughed. "I promise. I'm coming back tomorrow ... Robert." Robert Small chuckled softly. "Excellent. Just simply excellent!" He knew he would have to challenge her to keep her. He was already putting thought into how to ensure just that!

* * *

After checking Robert's out tray for the approved purchase orders and filing them in the appropriate binders in his office, Courtney packed up for the day. Walking past the fountain in the center of the department, she stopped to look at the two koi that swam lazily around the rocks in the pond. Beside the pool was a container of food. She opened the container and dropped a few pellets into the water. The koi demolished the morsels of food. She was unsure as to the significance of the fish, but knew she felt some strange connection to them. She had read a book on Fen Shui and knew that the flowing water brought inner tranquility to its surroundings. She wondered what significance, if any, the two fish brought?

Heading for the subway, she thought about how quickly her day had passed. She sat in a daze on the way home, and was relieved when the westbound train approached the Old Mill Station. The short bus ride to the apartment allowed her to reflect on all that had happened to her since her arrival in the city. When she saw her stop in front of her apartment, she felt happy to be back in front of her new home, even though it was in contrast to her new, posh work environment. She knew that now, she would have a steady income for at least six months, and she would be able to purchase a few necessary things for the apartment. She would survive, at least temporarily.

Courtney's thoughts returned to Jack. She felt more than a little silly about the conversation she had with him the night before. She wondered if she should call him and let him know about the job. He had been awfully nice to her despite the fact that she wasn't thrilled about his profession. She decided she would just leave a message for him on his cell phone. "Hi. Jack? This is Courtney ... Myers ... calling. I'm just calling to thank you for all you have done for me and, well, to let you know ... I got a job! Anyway, I just wanted to let you know that everything has worked out great and I appreciate everything that you have done for me! Thanks again, Jack. Bye ... for now." Courtney hung up the phone. Her hands were trembling slightly. She was more than a little nervous about the call.

As Courtney opened the fridge to see what she had to eat for dinner, the telephone rang. "Hey, hey, hey!" It was Jack. "You did it! I knew you would. Have you eaten?" Courtney was a little surprised by the question. "Well, actually, I was just rummaging through the fridge." Jack told her she could stop rummaging. "I'll be by shortly with a celebratory dinner!" Courtney was at a loss for words. This was certainly not what she intended. She told him it wasn't necessary. "Yes. I know it's not necessary, but I would like to see you one more time, if only to say congratulations in person. Do you have a problem with that?" he asked jokingly. She answered nervously. "No, no! That's great. Come on over."

Courtney decided to have a quick shower. Something about the words *one more time* had bothered her. Refreshed from the shower, she slipped into a short navy skirt and a white t-shirt and wiped a large circle in the steamy bathroom mirror. She was always relieved when her reflection appeared. She lightly applied some mascara to her long black lashes that served to enhance the deep rich brown of her eyes. Soft pink lipstick seemed to add to the gentle fullness of her lips. "What am I doing? I'm treating this like a date!" She debated about wiping the lipstick off when the buzzer sounded. "God. That was quick," she said running for the intercom. "Hey!" he announced. She buzzed him into the building. Courtney quickly ran back to the bathroom and brushed her long wet hair.

A soft rhythm beat on the door. When Courtney opened the door she was surprised that his arms were loaded with two paper bags. An amazing smell emanated from the bags and wafted into her kitchen. In the middle of the two bags was a beautiful bouquet of different colored lilies and a frosty bottle of white wine. "Oh, what have you done here? Let me help you." Jack smiled down at her. "Yes. I debated about the flowers. I didn't want you to think that this was a date. I just wanted to make your celebration special." Courtney laughed mostly at the irony of 'the date' comment. "Well, you've succeeded. What's in the bags?"

Jack put the bags of food on the kitchen table and removed the two individually wrapped aluminum plates. "I stopped by the restaurant. By the way, Paula says 'hi' and 'congratulations'. It's homemade veal Marsala with some sort of pasta." Courtney told him it smelled amazing. As Courtney handed Jack the glasses and corkscrew, she also set out to find some sort of vase for the flowers. She settled on a large beer glass that had been compliments of 'Charlie's'. "This is really nice of you, Jack." As he smiled and leaned lazily back in his chair, Courtney thought that he looked particularly sexy in his faded jeans and black t-shirt. Her eyes rested on his hands. She imagined his hands were those of an artist, full of expression. She continued to watch his hands as they carefully unwrapped the dinners. They didn't seem to match the macho image he exuded.

Courtney blushed as she looked down into the eyes that were now intently watching her. He had a look on his face that affected her deeply. She looked nervously back at the bouquet that she was putting in the glass. She hoped he didn't realize that he was having an affect on her. As she turned, she looked at the eyes of the Ouendat chief. Except for the color, his eyes were those of Jack. A shudder ran through her body.

Sitting down to the delicious meal that Paula had so lovingly packed, she tried to put the similarity of the Indian Chief's eyes and Jack's, in the back of her mind. Jack broke the silence by asking Courtney to tell him about the job? Although a little embarrassed about the simplicity of her role, Courtney elaborated on the posh surroundings of her new work environment and the kind nature of Robert Small and Anita. She talked at length about the role of the purchasing department. "People like to know that when they visit the other units, they will experience consistency of product. That is why there is a centralized purchasing department."

As she continued, Jack was impressed by the information that Courtney had accumulated during her first day on the job. "I'm pretty excited. I'm glad I can make a small difference to the efficiency of the department. Oh Jack, it's such a beautiful hotel." Courtney seemed proud of her new job and of the hotel that she now worked for. "Yes, and it just got a little more beautiful." Courtney could feel her cheeks flush in reaction to the compliment.

After dinner, Courtney led Jack into the living room. "Hey, great curtains." Courtney told Jack they were just temporary. She told him how she had made them from bed sheets. "Beautiful and crafty. Well, you'll make some man very lucky!" Courtney's face went suddenly sad. "Oh God, I'm sorry. I wasn't thinking. I only meant that you are beautiful and talented. If anything, that Brad guy is the loser for not having seen that." Jack was looking deeply into Courtney's eyes. "I believe in fate. You're here because something wonderful, beyond your wildest dreams will happen to you." Courtney laughed a gentle laugh. "Were you a fortune teller in a previous life, Jack?" Jack laughed. "Maybe I was, but who knows? Maybe even an Ouendat like you?" The comment confused Courtney. She thought back to Strong-Feather. She thought about how difficult her life had been. "I doubt that," she said seriously.

It was Jack who finally initiated the good-byes. "Well, we both have early mornings. Oh, I almost forgot. I got something for you, but it's in the car. Why don't you walk me out?" Courtney was surprised that Jack had bought her something else. "Don't tell me it's another plant?" Laughing, Jack said, "No, but you'll see."

They rode in silence in the elevator down to the parking lot. Courtney found herself lost in a myriad of emotion. She was thinking that Jack was really quite a nice person and he had turned into a good friend. However, she was thankful that there was someone else in his life. The fact that he was a police officer ended her debate as to whether she should take the relationship a step further. Yet, the conversation she had initiated with him the night before disturbed her.

As they approached Jack's car, he opened the driver-side door and reached across to the passenger seat. "Close your eyes," he commanded softly. Courtney obliged, her heart pounding in her chest. As she opened her eyes, Courtney was surprised to see that Jack had bought her a small leather bound day timer. "All great business people need one." Courtney felt overwhelmed by the gift. "Oh my God, Jack. It's great! I just love it. I don't know what to say?" Courtney gingerly unclasped the front of the gift and flipped through the crisp pages. She could feel tears forming in her eyes. "Thank you. It's perfect." Without thinking, Courtney reached up and kissed Jack softly on the cheek. She quickly shifted her focus back on the book.

He was dangerously close to her and she was relieved when he broke the awkwardness between them. "Well, it was worth the reward. Look ... I have to get going. Oh, by the way, my number's in there. I'd like to hear from you, once you're a little more settled in your job." Jack didn't give her a chance to respond. He settled into the driver seat and put his hand up in a gesture of good-bye. Courtney reciprocated by putting her hand up as well. She had thought it was the end. He had said he would like to hear from her again, leaving the door open once more.

* * *

As Courtney turned to walk back to the building, she was surprised to see Joe standing inside the glass doors of the entrance from the parking lot. She wondered how much of the exchange Joe had seen. Her question was answered as Joe opened the locked doors for her. "That's quite the COUSIN you have there." Joe winked. At first, Courtney was unsure of what to say. "He ... he was just congratulating me on my new job." Joe seemed genuinely excited. She briefly filled him in on her new job. "Well, I have to go look through my sad wardrobe, Joe." Courtney hesitated. "By the way Joe, I just wanted to thank you for all you've done for me." Joe insisted that it was nothing. "You a nice girl. If I was you, I'd keep that cousin of yours." Blushing, she thanked the little man for the advice.

Courtney spent the balance of the evening looking through her wardrobe. Most of her clothes were casual in nature and just wouldn't do for working at the upscale hotel. She would look around downtown the next day for a few simple items to supplement her wardrobe. She sat down to write out a budget to see just how much she could afford, but her mind wasn't focusing at all well on the task. It kept traveling back to Jack. She couldn't deny that he was physically attractive to her and she kept thinking of his strong arms and how sexy he had appeared when he lazily leaned back in her kitchen chair. She admonished her thoughts. "This is bloody ridiculous! It's just a stupid rebound!" She would have to stop thinking of Jack this way. "I'll only get hurt again." She picked up the day timer that he had bought her. She wondered how he had time to get dinner, wine, flowers, and buy the day timer too.

Courtney flipped to the page where Jack had written in his phone number. She knew the number was different from the cell number that he had given her before. It was obviously his home phone number. She thought it strange that he would take the chance of her calling when his girlfriend could be there. She also believed that if his girlfriend knew about the plant, the day timer, the flowers, the wine and the dinners, she wouldn't be particularly thrilled. Either this woman was a saint, or she was terribly unaware of the relationship that was developing between her boyfriend and another woman. Courtney found herself dialing the number.

"Well, hello there. Don't tell me you miss me already?" Courtney hadn't spoken yet. She realized he must have call display on his phone. "Well ... yes ... a little." Courtney was still flustered at his recognition of her telephone number and further surprised by a feeling that she did indeed miss him. "Jack ... I just called to say thanks. I'm so touched by all you have done for me. You're a really nice guy." Courtney was initially greeted by silence on the other end of the phone. "Oh, I'm not always a nice guy, Courtney." His deep laugh inexplicably affected her. Courtney was thinking back to how sexy she had found him that evening and how she had secretly wondered what it would be like to have his gentle hands caressing her.

She wondered how much she should say to Jack. Her thoughts of his girlfriend nagged at her mind. She didn't really want to cause problems for him. "Well, I think you're nice ... and pretty good looking. I'd say your girlfriend is pretty lucky." There was a sobering silence on the phone. "Well, maybe you'd like to tell her that? I could give you her number." Courtney could tell he was kidding, but something was eating away at her. Maybe it was the thought of talking to this other woman. "Jack, I don't care how understanding you say your girlfriend is, I somehow doubt she would take too kindly to my admitting that I find you attractive." Courtney could envision the smug smile on Jack's face. "So, you find me attractive do you?" Frustrated by the conversation, Courtney said, "Oh, this isn't going the way I wanted." Jack laughed the sexy deep laugh, once again. "Well, maybe you'd better go before you dig yourself in deeper." Courtney agreed. As she hung up the phone, she wondered what she had just done. She knew she had just told him that she found him attractive. "Oh, God!" Courtney covered her face with her hands. She had crossed the line, again. It was a line she had drawn. "What did I just say?" Her heart was beating rapidly. She felt an excitement that she attempted to control, but for some reason was having tremendous difficulty doing just that.

* * *

Courtney imagined that Jack O'Brien was smiling at the flirtatious nature of the call. He was probably wondering what thoughts were going through her mind at that particular moment. He would be puzzled by his own thoughts of her. From the moment he had spotted her, she had affected him. He probably knew he had startled her from the start, but she had startled him. He probably felt captivated by her Cinderella story. He would want to continue to be a part of the story, but would begin to think that it wasn't his right. The situation was becoming more complicated. "It's a rebound. It's simply not right."

* * *

Courtney attempted to focus on a budget for the upcoming weeks. She figured she would only be able to spend three hundred dollars supplementing her wardrobe. It wasn't very much, but if she could get by for the next month or two, she would be able to further budget for clothes after that. She would have to spend her money wisely.

As she lay down on the couch, her mind swirled with all that had happened. Eventually caught between the worlds of awake and asleep, she pictured herself kissing Jack on the cheek in the parking lot. A gentle wind blew. The parking lot was no more. They were standing beside a field of corn stalks. The wind caused the stalks to sway gently. As their golden leaves touched, they rustled softly. Jack's hand laced through her long black hair. His other hand encircled her waist and pulled her close. She could feel his strength pressing hard against her body. His grip tightened and suddenly the breath left her body. She ran a hand along his face, but it was the face of a stranger. Tears flowed softly from her visionless eyes. He whispered in her ear. She could sense relief from the words he had spoken, but felt damaged by her lack of sight. What could she offer him? She would only be a burden. She knew she would have to go with him. He held her closer, still.

The redness of blood blurred her vision. The black hollow of the mask's eyes caused her to scream. Courtney awoke in fear, her body soaked in sweat. They were being watched.

* * *

Tired from her fractured sleep of the evening before, Courtney summoned enough energy to go downtown. She made her way to the bank located in the hotel concourse. After opening a checking account, she arrived in the office fifteen minutes early. Robert Small came out of his office. "You're back ... and early to boot!" He looked skyward and pretended to thank God, as he often did. Courtney laughed and Robert continued. "I'm going for coffee. Why don't you tag along? I'll show you where the kitchen is." Robert Small led the way. On the way to the staff kitchen, he introduced her to several people. Courtney attempted to remember their names, but knew it was going to be difficult to remember them all. "Robert. Why are all of the departments located up here and Personnel is in the basement?" He explained that typically in hotels, the personnel department is where the public could easily access it. We do have a Human Resource department up here, but they deal in training programs and the hiring of specialized staff for all of the units. An example of that would be our chefs. Not only do guests want a consistency of environment but they also expect consistency when it comes to the quality and type of meal preparation. Our chefs are some of the best in the world."

The large staff kitchen surprised Courtney. Robert Small led her to the coffee pots located beside the double sink. "You might want to bring in your own mug," he said rummaging through a cupboard for one that looked like it didn't belong to anyone. He brought out a navy mug with gold lettering that simply read 'RYH'. "Here ... use this one for now." Courtney thanked him.

Once back in the department, Robert Small asked her if she could bring her coffee into his office. Courtney obliged. "I just wanted to apologize for not taking the time to properly interview you." Courtney smiled at him. "That's okay. There's really not all that much to tell. Maybe if you had of interviewed me properly, you wouldn't have wanted to hire me." The gray haired man reciprocated her smile. "Well, I doubt that. Tell me why you think that?" Courtney was extremely hesitant to open up about the details of her personal life, but told him about having just moved to Toronto and the sparse state of her new apartment. "I'm really thankful to have this job." She laughed softly. "Maybe I'll even get a bed because of it." Robert Small was taken by the young woman's independent nature and had taken a somewhat fatherly interest in her. "I like your initiative, my dear. We all have to start somewhere. Boy, I could tell you some stories about when I first started out!" Courtney thanked him for the compliment and wished he would tell her his story to success. "Speaking of initiative," Courtney began, "I guess I should be getting to those purchase orders." Robert Small agreed. "Yes. I guess that's a good idea." Courtney left his office, feeling even better about working for the kind man.

Courtney was still working on the paperwork on her desk, when Anita arrived in front of her. "Hey, are we still on for lunch?" Courtney was happy to see her. "Yes. Absolutely." Courtney would enjoy picking Anita's brain about the department and the role of the purchasing agents. "He wants me to go from noon until one. Is that okay?" Anita agreed that would be fine. "I'll see you then, unless you need anything."

The morning passed quickly. Anita arrived a few minutes before noon for her lunch with Courtney. She took her to a little Chinese restaurant located in the concourse. Courtney asked Anita if they could stop in a couple of clothing stores that they passed on the way. "Anita, my wardrobe desperately needs a makeover. I need to go on one of those television shows where they give you money to recreate a new wardrobe!" Anita laughed and leaning in towards Courtney whispered, "Can you keep a secret?" Courtney agreed that she could. "I buy a lot of my clothes at second hand stores. There is one called Phase II Designs. It's in the west end. There are lots of places like that all over Toronto. You can't believe the deals. A lot of it is designer stuff and some of it hasn't even been worn." Courtney smiled and thanked Anita for the idea. "From now on, you'll be checking out what I'm wearing and I'll be checking out what you're wearing." Anita laughed. "Ah yes, but I can keep the secret." Courtney was really starting to like this woman. In many ways, she reminded her of Jodie. She thought about how desperately she needed to try and reach Jodie.

After lunch, Courtney went back to tackle the work that was still piled on her desk. By the end of the day, she had greatly diminished the pile of purchase orders and she was happy that she was making some progress on the stack of paperwork. Robert Small had noticed the dwindling pile and started putting some thought into other things that Courtney could be doing for the department. He would ask Courtney to see him before the end of the day.

Courtney entered his office, just after five o'clock. He gestured towards one of the two leather chairs that pied out from his desk. "Courtney, I'm a little concerned, that once you're all caught up on those purchase orders, you'll be a tad bored with your position. I wanted to know if you would like to take on some additional responsibilities once you're caught up." Courtney was thrilled that Robert Small had asked her the question. "Absolutely," she offered enthusiastically. Her boss continued. "I'm having a staff meeting tomorrow with the agents. I'd like you to be present. I'll be asking them for their input to help find things to keep you busy. Courtney, I don't want to lose you, because the way things are going, you'll probably become bored, my dear." Courtney was beaming with the compliment and the endearment. "Thank you ... Robert."

* * *

Courtney was still beaming when she left the hotel for the day. Anita had told her that the clothing store was at Jane Street. The Jane subway stop was on her way home. She had little difficulty finding the store, as it was surprisingly quite large. Courtney was overwhelmed by the selection of inexpensive designer clothes. She rummaged through several racks and by the time she left, she had bought a navy suit, five tops, five skirts and two business jackets. She decided that she wanted to find some shoes to go with her purchases and ended up at a shoe store located up the street from the clothing store. The shoe store proved to be a success, as she bought two pairs of shoes to go with her clothing purchases. She asked the storeowner if she could leave the shoeboxes. She was thankful that he let her. She had five other bags to contend with on her ride back to the apartment and the boxes would prove further cumbersome on the bus that was still packed with rush hour passengers.

As Courtney stepped from the bus, she was shocked to see Jack standing in front of the building. He was with Joe. Both men smiled at her when they saw the fruits of her shopping excursion. "Here, let me help you?" Jack extended a hand to help. "Oh, thanks!" She wanted to ask him what he was doing there, but didn't want to create any more suspicion about the nature of their relationship in front of Joe. Joe helped by opening the front door for the couple. He was laughing at the volume of Courtney's purchases. "Just like a woman, Jack. I hope you keep enough for rent?" Courtney smiled. "Well, at least for one more month, Joe." All three of them laughed. "By the way Joe. Can I keep the couch for a while longer? I'm going to be wearing my new one, for a while." Joe told her to consider the couch a gift. "It suits you." Courtney was unsure at to whether that was a compliment or not. Joe read her thoughts. "All I mean is that it finally found a home, not that it's ugly or anything." Laughing, Courtney thanked him for his gift.

As Jack and Courtney stepped on the elevator and the doors finally closed, she asked the question that had been plaguing her. "Jack, as happy as I am to see you, why are you here?" A lazy smile spread across his face. "Well, I guess I should come up with some excuse as to how I just happened to be in the neighborhood, but I imagine you're just too smart for that. Would you believe I'm finding myself a little intoxicated by your rags to riches story?" Courtney looked nervously at her new purchases. She was unsure as to what to say. "Well, since you're here, I need some help. I need a bed. Do you know where I can get one?" Courtney had decided that the bed that Brad had got her could stay in the old apartment. It would bother her to sleep on the bed that they had once shared. Jack's smile broadened. Courtney read his thoughts. "Jack!" she exclaimed. She punched him in the arm. "Ouch!" He pretended to be hurt by the blow and rubbed his arm gingerly. "Yes, I think I can help you find a bed." Courtney looked skyward in mock frustration. "Come on. I'll make you a sandwich and then we'll go shopping … to a store!"

* * *

They took Jack's car to a store that sold all types of furniture and appliances. Although Courtney thought she would be more comfortable taking her car, she agreed that Jack knew the way and as it involved some highway driving, she realized that it made more sense for him to drive. Jack talked a little bit about why he had become a police officer. "I just always wanted to be a cop. My parents, however, wanted me to stay in the family business." Courtney asked if they were disappointed with his choice. "Sure they were. The problem with childhood and youth is that we spend the rest of our lives wondering what happened during those early years to make us who we are later on in life. I feel unsettled, at times. Yes. I'm quite sure I've disappointed them, but they would never say that." Courtney smiled at Jack. She understood exactly how he felt.

Courtney was thankful that Jack changed the subject. "Tell me some of the things that make you happy?" She thought seriously about the question. "Well ... I like water. I would like to live near water. I love the outdoors. Someday, I'd like to have my very own garden. I would grow my very own vegetables." It was Jack's turn to smile at Courtney. She knew he was thinking. It probably was a gentle vision that invaded his mind.

"Okay, it's your turn Jack!" Jack cleared his throat before starting. "Well, I like the wind on my face. I imagine I'd like to own a sailboat someday or ... at the very least, a convertible." He was laughing that deep rich laugh that she now enjoyed. "I like to sit in a comfortable chair and read a great book. I like people. I find them fascinating. People are so wonderfully contradictory; simple and yet so terribly complicated. Oh, and of course, there would be children. They are so tremendously honest." Courtney found herself enjoying the conversation, although she kept reminding herself not to get attached. He was spoken for, and even if he wasn't, he'd only end up hurting her. "So, kids eh? You must have nieces and nephews?" Jack told her he had nine and proceeded to name them. "They're pretty great. It would be wonderful to bring a child into this world and to nurture and love them. Yes, I can hardly wait until I have some of my very own." Courtney thought it was odd that this was one conversation that her and Brad had never had. Here she was with a virtual stranger and she knew more about how he felt about children then she had with the man she was going to marry.

THE RED MASK

Jack shot her back to reality. "What about you? Do you plan to have children?" Courtney fumbled with her words. "Yes. I imagine ... with the right man." Jack laughed. "Oh, you'll find the right man, if he doesn't find you first!" Courtney looked at him inquiringly. "Hey!" Jack had interrupted her thoughts. "We're here! Let's get you on a bed!" He laughed at his own joke. "You wish," she said. "Maybe I do, maybe I don't." Courtney shot back. "You keep that up and I will just have to call your girlfriend." Putting his car in park, he said, "Oh, I don't think you'll want to do that." He jumped out of the car before Courtney could say anything else.

Courtney had a hard time keeping up to Jack as they entered the large furniture store. Showroom after showroom greeted them until they finally arrived in the bedroom section. There was a wide selection of beds and Courtney fell in love with several of them. Realistically, she knew they were also widely out of her price range. "Jack. I'm on a pretty tight budget. I'm really just looking for something affordable. Anything would seem comfortable after my air mattress and the ugly couch." Jack led Courtney to the mattress section. Jack saw the salesman in the back of the showroom. He led Courtney over to him. Jack did the talking. "Excuse me. We're looking for the best double mattress and box spring for the cheapest price. We don't have time to negotiate. Do you have something reasonable?" Courtney was impressed by Jack's honest no-nonsense approach. However, the salesman seemed totally unimpressed. He did suggest a set at a price that Courtney felt she could afford. They settled on fifty dollars for a steel frame. The salesman proudly announced that delivery was free. Courtney was happy about that. "Jack, I need a lamp for the bedroom. It's pitch dark in there. The overhead light doesn't work." Courtney also ended up buying an inexpensive standup lamp for her bedroom.

After settling on delivery for the next day, and paying for her purchases, Jack insisted that Courtney bring the lamp home in his car. They managed to slide the lamp between the two front seats and Courtney held the shade on her lap. "Once again, it seems I'm indebted to you for your kindness." Courtney was surprised that when they got back to the building, Jack asked if she could manage the lamp. "Aren't you coming up?" Jack said he hadn't planned on it. "Oh, come on up for a cup of tea. I think I even have a little wine left, if you like? Please." For some reason, she didn't want him to leave. "For a bit then," Jack offered.

Courtney put the lamp temporarily in the living room beside the couch. Jack fished a light bulb out of the broken overhead light in the bedroom. As the light illuminated the living room with a soft glow, Courtney had a look of sheer excitement on her face. She turned and was surprised at the way Jack was looking her. He must have thought she was nuts to be so excited about a light. "Courtney. You're quite beautiful." Courtney felt a flutter in her stomach. "Jack. I'm not sure what's happening here?" Jack took a step closer to her. "I think maybe you know what's happening here." Jack's body was within inches of hers. "Look. I don't mess around with guys that are already spoken for, and I'm still not sure that any relationship, other than friendship, wouldn't be a big mistake for me." She wanted desperately to run into his arms and feel the power of his body surround hers. She was fighting hard to be in control. She even closed her eyes for several seconds, when she felt her resolve weakening. The strength of the energy between them was overpowering.

It was Jack who finally stepped back. "Friends, it is! I can certainly live with that." Courtney felt that she wanted him even more now that he had made it clear that he could handle a platonic arrangement. Courtney wondered aloud, "I don't know if I can?" Jack smiled. "Sure you can, Courtney." Jack went to the fridge and poured the remainder of the wine into two glasses. "A toast then. To two good friends!" As the glasses chimed, Courtney knew she still wanted him desperately. She could feel the ache in her stomach for him. She begged God to get her through the remainder of the evening with Jack. She knew Jack could sense her struggle. After swallowing his wine, he said that he had better call it a night. Courtney looked so relieved that he almost laughed out loud. "I'll drop by on Saturday to make sure the bed arrived okay." Courtney would have agreed to almost anything just to have the temptation of Jack's presence removed from her apartment. "Great. Great, I'll see you then. Saturday, it is!" Relieved, Courtney closed the door, after Jack disappeared.

Chapter 5

"Oh, ma cherie!" Tes yeux?" A tear fell down Strong-Feather's cheek. Francois Berthon gently brushed the tear away from his young lover's face. "Oh, ma cherie!" The young couple hugged amongst the whistling corn stalks.

The medicine man had put a powder in her eyes, taking away her vision. "I will take you away. We must leave this awful place. We will die here!" Strong-Feather melted in his arms. She wanted to leave with him, but she would be a burden. "Je ne sais pas?" she said indicating that she didn't know what she should do. "You must come with me. You will die here. Quel est ton desire?" She hesitated and then told him she would go with him.

* * *

Courtney woke up early the next day and picked out a long navy skirt and crisp white shirt from her new wardrobe. She was pleased with the look, as she tied her long dark hair up in a high ponytail. After applying a light coat of mascara and a darker red lipstick to her lips, she grabbed her purse and new day timer and headed off to her third day at work. It was Friday. She had such an inner excitement about the day that she couldn't even eat that morning. Maybe it was the arrival of her new bed that was causing her excitement? She had a deeper sense that her life was on a much different path than weeks earlier. Before leaving the building, she stopped by Joe and Maria's apartment. She made arrangements with Joe to accept delivery of the bed and to arrange for it to be put in her apartment. It would be so wonderful to finally have a bed to sleep on.

Courtney arrived at the office fifteen minutes before nine o'clock. Robert Small appeared shortly after. "Courtney! Come with me. I have something to show you." He led her to a small storage room located at the back of the office. "What's this?" Courtney asked. "It's our file storage room and, well, basic junk room. It's in desperate need of re-organization. Maybe it can be one of your projects? Jackie just never got around to it. It's not critical, but in the coming weeks, if you find you're short of things to do, maybe you can make a start on organizing it?" Courtney was pleased with the project. "That's not the only reason I wanted you to see this though. There are some old boxes of samples that you're welcome to rummage through. I know you're just starting out, and I thought there might be some things you would like for your new apartment." Robert Small ripped open one of the taped boxes. "There should be sheets, towels, curtains, whatever you like. Anyway, have a look through. It's just stuff we've accumulated over the years from suppliers. In an attempt to get our business, they often send tons of samples for us to peruse."

Courtney was quite touched that Mr. Small had thought of these things for her. "Oh my, this is great! Thank you so much. I'll have a look through them after work today." Robert Small looked pleased. Courtney couldn't help but think of how generous everyone had been and her thoughts went back to Jack. Courtney told Mr. Small about her new bed. "Well, there should be some sheets in there? I don't know, but you have a look." Courtney thanked him, again.

"Come on Courtney, we have a staff meeting in a few minutes." Courtney asked him if she could grab him a coffee. "Sure." He was thrilled by the offer but quickly added, "Well, only if you're going?" Courtney didn't really want a coffee, but told him she was going anyway. After the purchasing agents poured into the conference room, Robert Small reintroduced Courtney to the group. "As you know, Courtney Myers has joined us for the duration of Jackie's maternity leave and, quite frankly, I'm happy she has!" Everyone smiled and nodded appreciatively. "It won't be long, by the look of things, before Courtney has those purchase orders under control and then it will just become a maintenance issue. We would like to be able to keep her as busy as possible through her tenure with us. I would ask each of you to try and think of things that we can add to Courtney's responsibilities to help keep her busy and challenged."

Once again, the group all nodded and smiled. "If you have any suggestions, please bring them to my attention. Now, let's discuss what's happening on the purchasing end of things!"

The meeting lasted for forty-five minutes and Courtney learned a great deal about the role of the department. They discussed difficulties with certain suppliers, renovations within certain hotels, new products, and delivery timelines to all of the units. Courtney was fascinated with the whole meeting. After Robert Small adjourned the meeting, he asked Courtney if she had learned anything. "Oh, Yes! It's all so interesting." Robert Small was taken with her enthusiasm. "Good. Good!" She returned to her desk, feeling energized.

Courtney was tidying up her desk when Robert Small came by at the end of the day. She was surprised that he was leaving before her. "We're taking the family up north for the weekend." For some reason, she was surprised that he had children. Noting her surprise, he smiled and said, "Yes. Margie and I have two teenage daughters." Courtney wished Mr. Small a good weekend. "Yes. Good luck with the bed. Don't forget to have a look in those boxes." Courtney hadn't forgotten. After her boss left, she grabbed a footstool in the supply room and sat on it. She started rummaging through the boxes. Everything in the boxes was of the finest quality, and as tempted as she was to just take everything, she knew she couldn't possibly manage to get it all home on the subway. She ended up with two beautiful sheet sets of the finest cotton weave, a set of sheers for her bedroom and several heavy towels. She found two beautiful terry bathrobes and she immediately thought of Jack. He had done so much for her. She would love to give him one of the robes as a gesture of thanks. Courtney found some plastic hotel laundry bags on one of the shelves in the storage room and loaded her finds into the bags. She wondered what security would say if they saw her exiting the hotel with two large bags with 'Royal York Hotel' marked on them, but as she left the hotel, she didn't even encounter a raised eyebrow.

* * *

The subway was hot that day, but it wasn't particularly busy. Most people had already left for the weekend. Courtney endured the trip home and was thankful when she arrived safely at her apartment. After excitedly studying the box spring and mattress that Joe had put in the bedroom, she put the towels, sheets and Jack's robe in her linen closet. She hung the other robe up in her closet. She was overwhelmed at the quality of the large white terry robe and she fondled the inscription on the pocket, which was simply a gold embroidered 'RYH'. She held up the floor to ceiling sheers and marveled at how nice they would look once they were up. She thought she would hang them after she had something to eat. As she looked around at her still sparse apartment, she knew that it was starting to take shape. Once her bed was put together, her bedroom would officially be a bedroom! She thought about her dwindling finances and was thankful that next week would be a pay week. She would have to start curtailing her spending until she had a couple of paychecks in the bank. She was confident, however, that she would be able to get a handle on things.

Courtney went to the local Wal-Mart and bought the curtain rod she would need for her new bedroom sheers. She knew the sheers wouldn't be very dark, but they would just have to do until she could afford a blind for the room. Courtney also bought a navy bed skirt for her new bed. When she arrived back at the apartment, she was surprised by a knock at the door. It was Joe. "Everything okay with the bed?" Courtney thanked him for helping with the delivery. He insisted on helping her assemble the frame. Although she probably could have put it together herself, she was thankful for the help and knew that it made Joe feel like he was helping. With the box spring firmly on the frame, Courtney slipped the bed skirt over the box spring. Joe helped her lift the foam mattress on top. Courtney stood back with a pleased expression on her face. "Joe, I can't thank you enough for all of your help." Joe also insisted on putting up the curtain rod she had just purchased. Courtney felt like she should do something for Joe for all of his help. She went to the linen closet and pulled out two of the new thick towels that she had brought from the hotel. "These are for you and Maria for all of your help." Joe insisted that the gift wasn't necessary, but Courtney refused to take 'no' for an answer. "Okay. Maria will love. Thank you." Joe excused himself after graciously accepting the gift.

Courtney retrieved the new sheets from the linen closet and made

THE RED MASK

up the bed. It looked incredible. She pulled her old comforter out of her bedroom closet and put it on the bed. It didn't look incredible anymore. "Okay. I'll guess I'll have to splurge next paycheck!" she said. After the sheers were hung, Courtney surveyed the room from the doorway. She wished Jodie could see her new apartment. She decided that a call to her friend was long overdue.

She went to the telephone and quickly dialed Jodie's number. Her excitement increased when her friend answered the phone. "Hey girlfriend!" Jodie let out a gasp. "Courtney Myers! You are so in trouble with me! Where the hec are you? Why haven't you called me?" Courtney told Jodie she had tried and then proceeded to tell her the whole story of her relocation. "Oh, I'm so proud of you! I miss you desperately, though!" Courtney wished Jodie could be with her. "I miss you too, Jodie. Come visit me." Jodie said she would love to, but the weekend was out. "It's mom and dad's fortieth wedding anniversary. We're supposed to take them out for dinner." Courtney said that, of course, she understood.

"Jodie, I really like it here." Jodie told Courtney how happy she was for her. "By the way, who is he?" Courtney wasn't sure what Jodie was talking about? "Courtney, I'm talking about the cop that Brad is going on about!" Courtney was shocked. "Yep. He's telling everyone how he tried to get his stuff back and you've gone and shacked up with some cop. He said the guy threatened him." Courtney couldn't believe it.

"Oh, he's flipped, Jodie." Courtney told Jodie about how nice Jack had been. "Jodie, it was a lucky thing that Jack was here. He's just a friend I met here. Believe me, it's nothing more!" Jodie believed her. "Courtney, please be careful. Brad isn't going to let it go. He wants the ring!" Courtney was silent for a second. "I, ... I gave him the ring!" Jodie was thinking. "What is he up to?" Jodie had spoken the question that was in Courtney's mind. "I don't understand it, Jodie. Why can't he just leave me alone? For Pete's sake, HE ended things. He's acting like it was the other way around." Jodie felt badly for her friend and wished she could be there with her.

"Look Jodie, before I go, is there any more news up there on the burial ground?" Courtney wasn't sure why her mind had traveled to the ossuary. "Oh my, yes. They've discovered over two hundred bodies ... two hundred and twelve to be exact, or so the newspaper said. They found all kinds of artifacts; pottery, jewelry, masks. There are different native groups boycotting the removal of the skeletons and artifacts. Apparently, some had been removed initially, thrown into paper bags and taken to the museum. The native groups are in an uproar. It's dug up some deep feelings of disrespect of their culture. Pardon the pun!" Jodie chuckled. Courtney asked her what she knew about the masks. "I don't know anything about them. Maybe your mother knows more? She's involved." Courtney was truly surprised. It wasn't like her mother to get involved. Courtney would have to call her mother to find out more. "I'll call you Court, if I hear anything more." Before saying goodbye, Courtney gave Jodie her phone number and thanked her again for her concern over Brad.

After hanging up the phone, Courtney had a sudden impulse to go and lie on the new bed. She was suddenly overwhelmed with exhaustion. She lay on the bed for a long time pondering what Brad was up to? He seemed determined to interfere in her life. Courtney simply wished he would leave her alone and let her begin her new life. Her mind traveled back to the happier times they had. Slowly, Courtney's eyes began to close. *'Two hundred and twelve to be exact, two-one-two.'* Courtney's eyes sprang open in shock. Two-one-two was her apartment number!

* * *

Courtney was awoken by a distant knock at the door. She was groggy from oversleep and her stomach let out a deep hungry growl. She looked down and realized that she still had her clothes on from the night before. Courtney thought it was probably Joe or Jack at the door, so she struggled to the front door and looked out the peephole. She was shocked to see the distorted image of her parents standing in the hallway.

"Mom! Dad! Oh my goodness! Come in!" Courtney was happy that her bed had arrived before her unexpected visitors did. "Well, we thought we'd better find out what you've gotten yourself into here? We had to get your address from the phone company!" her father said, marching right past Courtney into the kitchen. Courtney's enthusiasm for the day had dwindled with the unexpected arrival of her parents. "Oh, I like the kitchen set," her mother piped in, "…and you have my picture!" Courtney fought to keep control of her nervousness. "Yes. I found it when I bought the kitchen set. It reminded me of home." Her mother smiled at the sentimentality of the picture. Courtney led her parents into the living room. Her father was staring wide-eyed at the orange and brown couch. Courtney read his mind. "Oh, don't worry dad. It's just temporary." Courtney lied about Joe's permanent donation to the apartment. "Through here is the bathroom and the bedroom. Her mother said the apartment was quite lovely. Her father just said, "It's kind of empty!" Courtney agreed. "Yes. I know it is dad, but I'm getting things slowly and it has been a tremendous amount of fun." She could sense that her father had more to say on the matter. "Fun, is it? Well when do you think you'll get a job to pay for all of this ... fun?"

Much to her father's surprise, Courtney told them about her new job. "The Royal York? I went to a conference there a few years ago. It's a pretty impressive place." Even her father couldn't fault her place of employment. Courtney felt an inner excitement that it was as close to a compliment as she would ever get in regard to her chosen field of work. "Yes. It's a pretty impressive place. I just love my job and my boss is just the greatest guy." Courtney's father raised a suspicious eyebrow. "Dad! He's your age for goodness sake! Look, I'll make a pot of tea. Come on in the kitchen." Her parents followed her back into the kitchen and sat at her new table. Suddenly, they all jumped as the intercom buzzed. Courtney pushed the listen button. "Hey! Do you have that bed yet? I'm ready to try it out!" Courtney closed her eyes in response to Jack's poor timing, but then a small smile crept across her face. "Come on up." Courtney thought, *'This should be interesting.'* She turned and saw her parents' shocked expressions. "Who the hell was that?" her father demanded. "Well, it's a long story, but you're about to meet Jack. He's just a friend. Don't go reading anything into this Dad!" Her father responded believing he had caught her in a lie. "Sure, just a friend, who's interested in your bed!" Eve Myers jumped in. "He's the one I told you about, dear."

Jack knocked a beat on the door and Courtney answered it. Initially focusing on Courtney's disheveled state; he didn't notice Mr. and Mrs. Myers sitting behind Courtney. "Hey beautiful. Is it here yet?" As Jack brushed by Courtney, she witnessed, with some pleasure, the obvious surprise on his face. "Jack. I'd like to introduce my parents." Jack's hesitation was brief. "Hello. Courtney, you should have said something. I can come back another time." Courtney's father didn't give her a chance to respond. "We wouldn't dream of it. Jack ... is it?" Courtney knew full well that her father hadn't forgotten Jack's name. He was simply toying with him. "Courtney was just making us some tea. Would you like a cup?" Jack had fully regained his composure. "Excellent ... love some." He had realized that he was under scrutiny. "You know how I take it, Courtney." Courtney did know and was enjoying that Jack was now toying with her father. She thought, once more, how this should be an interesting situation. Almost as interesting as when Jack had flashed his badge at Brad. "Why don't we sit in the living room," Courtney suggested. "I'll bring the tea in." As Courtney's parents rose to comply, Jack grabbed one of the wicker chairs and brought it into Courtney's living room. She was thankful that he did. Once again, he was taking charge of the situation.

Courtney could hear her mother speak in the next room. "So, ... tell us Jack. How exactly did you meet our daughter?" Jack laughed the deep familiar laugh that Courtney now enjoyed. "Well, Mrs. Myers, actually, I found her asleep in a park. I woke her up, found her an apartment and now, well, we're ... friends." Courtney could only imagine the look on her father's face. Courtney yelled from the kitchen. "Jack! Tell them the whole story. Dear God! You'll give my parents heart attacks!" As she entered the living room with her parents' teas, she looked at Jack. He smiled at her before continuing. "What? I did find you asleep in a park. I also woke you up and brought you here." Courtney opened her eyes wide and frowned at Jack. "Well ... let me start at the beginning. I'm a Toronto Police Officer. I found this beautiful young woman asleep in her car. I offered to assist her with her search for a suitable apartment. I've dropped in from time to time to make sure she's okay and settling in. The city can be overwhelming at first. I've simply tried to make sure she's taken care of. I assure you, I have no ulterior motive." There was a look of slight relief on both of Courtney's parents' faces. "Well then, I guess we should thank you." Courtney's father extended a hand that Jack shook. Courtney's mother piped in. "She's very precious to us. It's a relief to know that there is someone looking out for her." Courtney felt strangely like a child. *'I could have looked out for myself. I don't need a man to make sure I'm okay!'*

Jack was winning them over. They didn't question the relationship further. "Well, I really can't stay. I'll check on Courtney later, if that's okay?" Courtney watched as her parents nodded their approval. Courtney walked Jack to the door. "How did I do?" he asked. "Apparently, quite well! I ... I guess you'll be back." Jack smiled. "Sure. I'll be back later. Okay?" Jack bent and planted a soft kiss on her cheek. Courtney was confused by the gesture.

As she re-entered the living room, her father was standing thoughtfully by the sliding doors to her balcony. "He seems decent enough, Courtney. A little smug maybe, but decent enough." He opened the sliding glass doors and disappeared onto the balcony. Courtney's mother gave her a knowing smile. "Yes. He's also pretty good looking." Courtney couldn't help but smile back at her mother. "Yes. I've noticed that too, mom. However, he's quite spoken for." Courtney's mother had a hint of disappointment on her face. "Is there ANY chance?" Courtney asked her mother what she meant, knowing full well. "Well, of a romantic involvement." Courtney laughed. "No, mom. He's taken. He's really just a friend. Oh, and he's certainly not involved with another man!" Her mother laughed, as well. "Yes. I can see that now!" Courtney was relieved when the subject changed away from Jack O'Brien.

"Honey, your father and I are off to Florida next week. Your dad is golfing with some of his old cronies and I've agreed to tag along for the rest." Courtney told her mom it sounded wonderful. "Well, why don't you come? We could sneak down to the Keys. You know how I love that Hemingway house?" Courtney laughed. "I don't think that would go over very well at work, mom." Her mother looked disappointed. "Are there other wives going?" Her mother said there were, but they all golfed. "You know how I feel about golf. It spoils a perfectly good walk. Besides, they're kind of ... well, boring. Never mind. I'll take a few good books and wile away my hours." Courtney laughed. "Mom, you'll have new friends as soon as you get there." Her mother was still looking a little disappointed.

"Mom, I need a favor. I need you to pick up my vacuum and television. I will call my landlord but I'll need to return the extra key to the apartment. Can you drop it off, after you get those two things from the apartment?" Courtney felt a little guilty for having asked this of her mom. She was thinking that maybe she should have asked Jodie? "Of course honey. I don't mind." The fact that she had said she didn't mind meant that she had obviously questioned whether she should mind. Her mother could instill guilt without actually overtly doing it. It was just her way.

"Mom, I was talking to Jodie last night." Her mother smiled and said, "How is she?" "Good." Courtney answered. "She was telling me about the burial grounds. She said you were involved some how?" Eve Myers was pensive. "Oh, it's an awful situation. Everyone's bickering over what should be done. Some of the bones and artifacts were removed ... in paper bags of all things. It's just a crime. The ossuary is over three hundred and fifty years old. It was the time of Strong-Feather. Who knows? Maybe her father was among the poor souls. He was a chief, you know?" Sometimes Eve Myers' memory seemed to fail her. "Yes. I know mom."

Her father re-entered the living room. "Have you heard any more from Brad ... since the other night?" her mother asked. "No." Courtney filled them in with greater detail about the incident at the apartment. "Yes. Bill and I ran into each other the other day. He had mentioned that Brad was still upset over some things of his that you supposedly had. I told Bill that I didn't know anything about it." Courtney was surprised that Brad had continued to drag his father into his charade. "Well, I wish I hadn't thrown that stuff out. It's just that I was so hurt at the time. There wasn't anything of real value in the bag. I can't understand why he's continuing to cause so much trouble about it. He has the ring back! Although, Jodie told me he's apparently denying that fact!" Courtney continued. "It was really fortunate that Jack was here when Brad showed up." Courtney told her parents about the badges. Her mother's smile was broad. Her father's smile was more difficult to read. "It sounds like this Jack guy has come in handy." Courtney laughed. "Yes. He's turned into a pretty good friend." There was no way Courtney could elaborate on the mix of emotions she felt for Jack. She was thankful when the conversation drifted into another subject. Eventually promising that she would come up for dinner after they returned from vacation, Courtney's parents got ready to leave. She walked them to their car.

She felt a mixture of sadness and relief that they were leaving.

She hugged her father good bye and then stood in front of her mother. "Mom? Did the chief wear a mask?" Her mother went suddenly pale. "He was one of the few Ouendat that did. Why do you ask?" Courtney hesitated. "Was it red?" Eve Myers stood frozen in front of her daughter. "You've seen it. You've seen the mask," she whispered. Shock traveled through Courtney's body. "Why? Have you? Have you ... seen it?" A flash of fear crossed Eve Myers' face. "I did until I met your father. I don't know why it comes. In the time of the villages, a mask hung outside of the village on a pole. Visitors would know that the chief was in by seeing it. I imagined the red mask was his. I don't think it is a bad thing, but I don't know." Courtney's father jumped in. "Eve. Don't you get going on that crazy stuff? It's all hocus pocus, Courtney. Your mom thinks she married HER medicine man." Her father laughed at his own joke. Courtney stood pensive and then issued more hugs and kisses.

She felt relieved that the visit had gone fairly well. Her parents seemed more at ease with her decision and it took a huge strain off of her. She hadn't liked the feeling that she had disappointed them. Still, there was emptiness as she watched them drive away. She thought about the mask and it sent a chill through her body. *'This is crazy stuff'*, she thought. *'How could mom have seen the same mask?'* She didn't believe in the supernatural or spiritual awakening of the dead. That was simply not possible. The medicine man in her dream was evil. Despite their differences, Courtney knew her father wasn't evil. "It's all hocus pocus!" Courtney exclaimed.

* * *

Courtney returned to her apartment and flopped on the new bed. Her thoughts were still of the mask. She could have fallen asleep to allow her dreams to handle her thoughts, except that the phone was now ringing. She got up off of the bed and went to the living room to get the phone. "Thought I'd better call this time. What are you doing?" Jack asked. Courtney opted for the truth. "Actually, I was just trying out my new bed." Jack was silent for a second. "Well, that just conjured up an image." Courtney was starting to enjoy the flirtation. "Does it? Well, why don't you tell me about the image you have?" She could tell that she had caught him off guard by continuing the game. "I don't think you really want me to do that." Courtney laughed a sultry laugh. "How do you know what I want?" Courtney was unsure about what she was doing. Her heart was racing in her chest and she was excited about the feeling that had been generated.

Courtney took the phone back into the bedroom. "Hold on a second, Jack." She put the phone on the bed. Removing her clothes, she lay back on the bed. She put the phone back to her ear. "Okay, what am I doing now?" Jack was silent. "Jack?" Courtney ran her free hand down her naked body. "Jack, what am I doing now?" Jack finally spoke in a husky voice. "Dear God Woman! Don't toy with me! You know I could be there in about five minutes!" Courtney laughed. "I'll leave the door unlocked." Courtney disengaged the phone, before Jack's protestation.

* * *

Courtney was already wondering what she had started, for she knew that she had indeed started something. She needed him or, at the very least, needed to feel a man making love to her at that moment. She went to the bathroom and lightly sprayed perfume on her body. She brushed out her long hair. After a few minutes, the intercom buzzed in the kitchen. Courtney ran to buzz open the building door for Jack.

A moment later, she could hear him enter the apartment. "Courtney?" Courtney was silent as she lay on the bed, the Royal York robe draped invitingly over her body. As Jack entered the bedroom, their eyes connected. She could see the look of wanting on his face and it delighted her. Jack was attempting to control himself. Courtney felt concern over the obvious struggle she could see going on inside of him. "Aren't you going to join me?" she asked playfully. "Courtney, believe me, I want to. I don't think there is a man alive that wouldn't want to but …". Courtney knew Jack must have been thinking about his girlfriend. She was starting to feel self-conscious. "Jack, I need to be made love to." Jack folded his arms across his chest. "Yes. I can see that." Courtney asked, "Is this about Ellen?" Jack closed his eyes for a moment. "Partly. Look, why don't you put that robe on and we'll talk. I can't talk to you like this." Jack left the bedroom. Courtney was feeling more and more ridiculous about her obvious show of desire.

As Courtney entered the living room, Jack was standing by the sliding doors with his arms still folded defiantly across his chest. "Jack, don't you want me?" The silence seemed like an eternity for Courtney. "Would you like to feel how much I want you?" Courtney smiled. The question was redundant and Jack knew it. "Courtney ... I'm in a relationship." Courtney was undaunted by the bomb. Her desire had taken over her mind. She inched closer to Jack. "Stop. This isn't the way it should be." Courtney kept moving in on her prey. "What if it's the way I want it?" Courtney noticed Jack's jaw tighten. "Maybe, at this particular moment, you think you want it this way, but I don't believe you will after." Courtney was still undeterred. "Isn't that my decision to make?" Courtney slipped off the robe. Jack's eyes traveled down to the soft curves of her body. It was all too much for him. "Oh, God," he moaned.

With one swift movement, he reached an arm around her waist and pulled her into him. She could feel his desire pressing hard into her stomach. His other hand reached to the back of her neck, his fingers entwining themselves in her long black hair. He gently pulled her head back and his mouth captured hers. The kiss was hard but was softening as her tongue slipped gently into his mouth. He released her lips and kissed the nape of her neck that elicited a shudder through her body. He moved down her body with his gentle kisses. It was more than Courtney could endure. "Oh Jack," she murmured. He returned to full stance and swept Courtney up in his arms. As he carried her to the bedroom and laid her gently on the bed, he said, "Is this what you had in mind?" She watched in awe as he removed his shirt revealing the rippling muscles of his chest. She had never been with a man so well defined and the anticipation of his bare chest and body against hers was making her mad with desire. As Jack removed his jeans, she could see his desire under the navy boxers. She couldn't believe that a man could have this kind of affect on her.

Courtney let out a small cry of delight as Jack grabbed her up off of the bed and lifted her into his arms. Her legs automatically wrapped around his waist and he grasped her firmly. He gently laid her back on the bed and ran his strong hands through her hair. He whispered, "This isn't what I wanted." Courtney murmured rhythmically, "I know ... I know." Jack was moving on her. "What about love, Courtney?" Courtney couldn't think as her body ached for him to continue. "Are you in love with me, Courtney?" As Courtney remained silent, his desire seemed to intensify and the speed of his lovemaking increased. Courtney would have just about said anything at that moment. As his right hand traveled down between their bodies, she quickly realized that he was a masterful partner and she cried out her desire. He continued to work her until she couldn't stand it any more. "Yes!" He was smiling. "Yes, what?" Courtney panted the words between squeals of delight. "Yes. I could love you." They weren't the words he had wanted, but it was too late to turn back now! They let go of the passion they had elicited in each other. They lay silent. Jack propped himself on his forearms, so as not to hurt her with his physical size. He lifted his bowed head and looked deep into her dark eyes. She was looking pleadingly up at him for some sort of reassurance.

As he gently rolled over pulling her on top of him, he asked, "You could love me or you do love me?" Courtney smiled down at him. "I love what just happened between us?" The seriousness of Jack's look made her wonder what she should do or say now. "Jack, I think there are a couple of things to remember. First of all, you're involved with someone else. Secondly, you're a cop and I told myself I wouldn't fall in love with another man in your line of work." Jack didn't move but she could feel his muscles tense under her. "Well, Courtney. Let's eliminate the first problem." Courtney was looking at him surprised. "How the hec do we do that Jack? You love her don't you?" Jack answered. "I ended the relationship last week." Courtney was shocked. "What? Why didn't you tell me?" Jack rolled Courtney over so that he was, once again, on top of her. He didn't want her to run away from him. "I didn't tell you because it created a safe distance between us. I never expected this! I didn't think you would pursue anything as long as you thought there was another woman. I wanted your love for me to grow. If anything, I thought you would respect that, and her, and not let your desire get the better of you." Jack was silent for a moment. "Obviously, I underestimated your need." Courtney tried to squirm under him.

"Oh, you're not going anywhere. I'm not done yet." Jack held her one free hand firmly in his grasp.

"I think I fell for you the moment I saw you asleep in your car, but I could sense a distance because of what I do for a living. I'm sorry that's my career, but it is?" Courtney tried to squirm out of his grasp but he was too strong. "Let go of me," she cried. "Listen!" he said, "You listen to me now because you wouldn't listen to me before. I don't make a habit of making love to a woman without having her love me back, but I just did. So you can damn well listen to me now!" Courtney could sense that he had her beat and she gave up her fight to get out from beneath him. "I'm not Brad. I wouldn't hurt you that way. If I decided to make you my bride, I damn well would follow through. I don't think Brad's career choice makes him a jerk. I think he would be a jerk no matter what he did for a living! I'd like you to think about that before you admonish me from your life because of my career choice. That's not fair to me or for that matter ... to you!"

Courtney's eyes were angry. She didn't like being lectured or being told how she should feel, and she certainly didn't like the way that Jack had her pinned to the bed. Through gritted teeth, she asked if he was going to let her up now. He could see the fiery look in her eyes and knew that he hadn't won her over. "Yes. I'll let you up!" As Jack freed her hand, he wasn't ready for her hand coming up and hitting him hard across the face. Although it was meant as a slap, her nails crossed his cheek, leaving a deep scratch on his face. Jack felt the wound. He looked hard into her eyes. As he got off of the bed, he grabbed his clothes from the floor and threw on his boxers and jeans. Courtney lay in shocked silence at what she had done. She could see the anger begin to build in his eyes. She waited, afraid of what he might do. He surprised her by smiling. "Well, my little kitten needs to do some growing up! Call me when that happens." As Jack left the bedroom, Courtney struggled with an apology. "Jack, I ...". Seconds later, she heard the apartment door slam shut! Courtney fell back on the bed, feeling sick in her stomach. The tears started to stream down her face. "Oh God, what have I done?" she cried.

* * *

Courtney eventually cried herself into a deep exhaustive sleep. She was yelling at him to come back. "Jack, please come back. Oh no, please …". Courtney sat up quickly. Reality hit her. How could she have hit him so hard? "I'm such a stupid fool. I had him in the palm of my hand." Courtney tried to defend her actions. "I didn't like what he was saying." Courtney cried. "Oh God." She put a hand over her mouth. Her eyes closed with the weight of the disappointment she felt inside.

She grabbed the phone and dialed his cell number, but there was no answer. The message rang through. "Oh Jack. Please come back. I just can't imagine what came over me. I feel sick about it. Please Jack. Come back!" Courtney hung up the phone. She quickly picked it up again and dialed Jack's home number. She was, once again, greeted by the answering machine. "Jack, I left a message on your cell. We need to talk. Please call me back. Please?"

Courtney sat and thought hard about why she had lashed out at Jack. It was totally out of character for her. She just couldn't come up with a reasonable reason why? She had especially hated the way he had pinned her to the bed making her listen to what he had to say. She finally felt that the slap was not at Jack at all, but at Brad. She knew it had been unfair to direct her anger at Jack, after he had just given her the most incredible gift of lovemaking she had ever experienced. She had treated him cruelly and hurt him deeply. She thought about his reluctance to make love to her and how she had seduced the end result. If the roles had of been reversed, she definitely wouldn't want to see that person again. She would scream abuse if a man ever slapped her! "Oh God! I've ruined everything! I was falling in love and I've foolishly ruined it for myself!"

Despite her continued attempts to reach Jack, there was no call back from him. Courtney couldn't help but go over and over everything that had happened between the two of them. One thing was certain; he had awoken a passion in her that she never knew existed. As she looked around at her apartment, it suddenly seemed emptier than ever. Her enthusiasm had left with Jack. As she sat on the orange and brown couch, she was deep in thought. "Oh my God! I love him! I must have him back!"

Chapter 6

Jack had driven all the way to Niagara in the dense fog. It seemed to strangely disappear as he started up the long paved driveway. Half way up the driveway, he saw his brother Pete coming around from the back of the old stone house. Pete was waving wildly at Jack. Jack was now smiling at the sight of his older brother. Pete greeted him with a hug and pat on the back. "Hey man! What brings you around? We thought you'd died or something?" Jack probably felt like part of him had. "Ya. Ya. Well don't start divvying up the inheritance five ways yet?" His brother let out a loud laugh. "What inheritance? Didn't you know mom and dad are off cruising the Caribbean spending it all?" At first, Jack thought his brother was kidding. "Hey, I'm serious. Dad bought mom a trip for their anniversary. They left for Miami yesterday. It's some seven day Caribbean deal." Although Jack was disappointed that he wouldn't see his parents, he was happy that they had finally decided to go on a trip. "Well, well. Good for them. It's about time!" Pete agreed. "Ya. You should have seen mom. She was a basket of nerves over the whole flying thing. Of course, they picked a great time to go. We had our first freeze last night." Jack knew that the first freeze signified the harvesting of the grapes for the making of the region's famous ice-wine. When the grapes froze their sugar content rose making them sweeter. The sweet dessert wine was world famous.

"Come on in, bro. Sheila is inside feeding the kids. They'll be so excited you're here." Sheila and Pete had two boys; Derek and Mathew. They were ruff and tumble boys and their antics often reminded Jack of when he grew up with his brothers. Jack followed Pete into the large stone house. The house also had a large stone basement that was originally a wine cellar. The basement had been converted into an apartment prior to the O'Brien purchase of the home. When they were first married, Pete and Sheila lived happily in the apartment. However, Jack's parents had insisted, with the birth of Derek, that Pete and Sheila needed to raise their grandchildren on the main floor of the home. The young couple had guiltily accepted the switch. Pete's parents were simply not going to take 'no' for an answer.

"Sheila! Come and see who's crept out of the woodwork!" As Sheila appeared and saw Jack, she ran up to him and gave him a big sisterly hug. "Hey, good looking. Where the hec have you been hiding?" Jack grabbed his sister-in-law in another big hug. "You know how it kills me to see you with him. How do you expect me to come here and sit in jealous agony?" Sheila let out a squeal of delight. "Oh, you smooth talker you. What would Ellen say if she heard you say that?" Noticing Jack's frown, she said, "You're still with Ellen right?" Jack had to admit the relationship was over. Sheila's face brightened. "Okay, who is she then?" Jack started to walk past Sheila, but stopped beside her and whispered, "You." Sheila turned red and hit Jack with the tea towel she had in her hand. Jack laughed. "Now where are my nephews?"

The two boys looked up from their lunch and ran across the kitchen yelling, "Uncle Jack! Uncle Jack!" Jack knelt down and wrapped his arms around the two little boys. "Hey you guys! What's up?" The boys talked non-stop about the awful lunch their mother was making them eat. "Well, let's see what we have going here?" Jack looked at the lunch of soup and sandwiches. "Looks pretty healthy to me." Mathew looked at his uncle. "Exactly!" he said. They all laughed.

"Join us, Jack," Sheila insisted. "Absolutely. I enjoy healthy food." Both boys were looking at their uncle with adoration. "You do?" Mathew asked. "Sure. How do you think I grew into such a strong man, if I didn't eat tons of healthy stuff that Nana made?" The boys begrudgingly started to eat their lunch in an attempt to grow big like their Uncle Jack. Sheila laughed. "Too bad you weren't here ten minutes ago. You would have saved me a lot of aggravation!" Suddenly Derek piped in. "Uncle Jack? If you ate the healthy stuff and grew big, then dad must have eaten all of the junk food." Jack let out a huge laugh. "Yes. Your dad ate tons of candy. Now that stuff is okay once in a while, but not all the time! He would have been a strapping man like me if he had of listened to Nana." Pete jumped into the conversation. "That's not quite true boys and that's enough Jack!"

The boys ended up demolishing their lunch, much to their mother's satisfaction. Jack watched as they ran off to play a new game on their computer. They asked him to come watch and he said he would after he caught up on things with their parents. Alone with Pete and Sheila, Jack asked about the business. Pete answered his brother. "This has been one of the most profitable years ever, Jack." The business had been quite lucrative over the years. The family was wealthy from the years of dedication and hard work in the business. Although Jack had felt guilty for leaving it, he was happy that his parents were now extremely wealthy and could finally afford to enjoy their lives outside of the business.

Sheila broke Jack's thoughts. "So Jack. What's news with you? What happened to you and Ellen?" Pete laughed. "Just like a woman to want to know the sordid details! It's probably been killing her." Jack forced a smile. "Well, it's pretty simple really. She just wasn't the woman for me." Sheila was still looking at Pete. "Who is she Jack?" Jack played dumb. "Who's who?" Sheila turned and looked at Jack disapprovingly. "You know who! The woman who has stolen your great big heart!" Jack knew his sister-in-law wasn't going to let it go. "Well, the woman who temporarily stole my heart was named Courtney, but don't get all excited Sheila. It ended before it really started." Sheila looked disappointed. "If I understand correctly, you left Ellen for Courtney, but then you ended things with Courtney? Men are such idiots!" Jack let out a sigh. "It's kind of complicated, Sheila." Sheila was undaunted by Jack's reluctance to elaborate. "What's so complicated about Courtney?" Jack really didn't want to get into the details. That wasn't why he felt he had come there. He was looking for a diversion from the phone messages he had received from her the day before. He really didn't want to spend his day off talking about Courtney.

Jack tried to change the subject. "So Sheila, how's motherhood? What are the boys up to these days?" Sheila looked perturbed. "Nice try, Jack!" Pete went to his brother's defense. "Sheila, I get the impression that Jack doesn't want to talk about this girl." Sheila looked at her husband with a peculiar expression. "You guys just don't get it. You lock it all up inside. You go into your caves. You think you can handle it. Well, sometimes it helps to open up a little bit and get some feedback from other people. Maybe you're looking at things one way, but need to look at things another way?" Jack smiled. "Okay Sheila! You win!"

Jack proceeded to tell Pete and Sheila the entire story of Courtney including the extent of the intimacy between them the day before. Pete said, "You're doing the right thing bro. Forget her. Any person who does that just isn't worth it!" Pete was pointing at the scratch along Jack's face. Sheila, on the other hand, was looking at her husband dumbfounded. "How can you say that Pete! Don't you remember the time when I expected you to propose and you didn't?" Sheila turned and looked at Jack. "We had even looked at wedding rings. Months passed and he still hadn't proposed. All of our friends were engaged or married. We went on a trip to California. I had expected that this was it. He would ask me on the trip. When he didn't, I was pretty upset. I shoved him pretty hard in frustration and he fell back and hit his head on the edge of the dresser in our hotel room." Pete was nodding. "Yes. That's true. I was so out of it after hitting my head, I asked her to marry me!" Pete was laughing now. Sheila frowned at her husband and then continued. "Jack, she probably feels just sick about it. Don't you think she's at least worth a phone call? Jack, what if you walk away from her and she's the one?" Your one and only! You should find out!"

Jack was running his hands through his hair. "Look, I didn't want to lay all of this stuff on you guys!" Pete laughed. "What's family for? Jack, I have to agree with Sheila." Sheila now smiled sweetly at her husband who continued. "You should find out if Courtney's the one who will sucker you into marriage." Sheila punched her husband hard in the arm. "See Jack! See how easy it is to be provoked!" They all laughed. Jack was thinking about what Pete and Sheila had said. He was thinking about whether Courtney was indeed his one and only. He had certainly thought so, the day before!

When he started the drive away from his parents' that evening, the situation with Courtney continued to plague him. Turning at the base of the driveway, he was surprised that it was foggy again. The

THE RED MASK

weather was strangely like his thoughts. His car disappeared into the wall of mist.

* * *

The train ride to the office was packed with Monday morning commuters. Courtney was trying desperately to put all that happened between her and Jack out of her mind. She would only try to focus on her work today, not on the disastrous situation she had created.

She threw her mind into her work. By the end of the day, she had completely cleared the desk and was proud of the accomplishment. "Courtney? Do you have a moment?" Robert Small was standing outside of this office. "Sure!" she answered. As she entered the office, Robert Small was flipping through one of the large black purchase order binders. "Have you ever used Excel?" Courtney admitted that she hadn't, but had taken a course in college that touched on the computer program. "It's pretty simple really. Each month, I do a report on purchases for the month. We can certainly add that to your job description. I'll show you tomorrow, if you like?" Courtney was pleased with the new responsibility, but her response was lacking her usual enthusiasm. Her boss looked up at her. "Is everything okay? You don't seem like yourself today." Courtney apologized. "Everything's great. I just didn't sleep particularly well last night. I'm sorry." Robert Small felt that wasn't the whole story, but knew he shouldn't pry further. "I recognize that it is more than we hired you for, but it'll give you some additional experience that may come in handy." Courtney was relieved that Robert Small had refocused on her increased responsibility.

As Courtney left the office that day, she was pleased that Robert had such faith in her. At the end of her tenure with the purchasing department, she hoped that she would have gained enough experience to make herself marketable in another position within the hotel. If not, she would be able to add some real work experience to her applications. She wanted desperately to share her accomplishment with Jack. He had been a real pillar of support since her move to Toronto. Her mind traveled back to the way his lips had traveled down her neck and the feeling that it had generated within her body. The thought of never having him make love to her again made her ache inside. She had realized over the past two days what a fool she had been. Jack was right! It wasn't Brad's job that made him a jerk. He just hadn't grown up as a person. It seemed that although Brad didn't want her, he also didn't want anyone else having her. She recognized that she, too, had some growing to do. She had spent the last forty-eight hours thinking hard about that fact! She decided, as hard as it would be, she would not call Jack. She would just have to wait. If she called him today, it would look like she hadn't put any thought into what had occurred. She would have to deny herself the privilege of speaking and sharing with him.

The workweek went well and as a reward for her hard work, she called Jack from the office. She dialed his cell number and her heart seemed to skip a beat when he answered the phone. "Jack here." Jack sounded gruff on the other end of the phone. "Hi Jack. It's Courtney." The only sound was the crackle of the phone line. Jack's manner was abrasive when he responded. "What do you want?" Courtney felt uncomfortable for having called. "Jack, I think we should talk?" Jack told her he had no interest in talking to her. "Jack, please. Don't shut me out. I really need to talk to you. If you decide after seeing me that you don't want to ever see me again, I'll respect that. Please, Jack?" The phone continued to crackle. "I don't see that it will do any good. It's too soon, Courtney." Jack exhaled slowly. Courtney broke the uncomfortable silence. "Look, I'll be home tomorrow night. If you come, you come. Jack, I hope you do." Courtney just wanted the uncomfortable conversation to end. "Jack, I will understand if you don't, but I really hope you do." Courtney hung up the phone.

* * *

Courtney lay wondering what Jack would do. Her mind was obsessed with making things work between them. She dreamt of the eventuality of him coming. Her dreams twisted back to the scratch she had inflicted on his face. It was no longer his face that she envisioned. The medicine man knew that she was leaving with the traveler. It would be wrong for the village. He had promised her mother that he would ensure that it didn't happen. He had put the powder in her eyes believing that if her eyesight were gone, the traveler would have no further interest in her. He would surely leave the village without the burden of a blind partner. He had watched her grow into the beautiful young woman. She had cast a spell on him and he had secretly hoped that she would some day be his. The threat of the Iroquois had taken away his dreams.

Strong-Feather had nervously waited for that night. They would escape under the cover of darkness. She would know when it came because the sun would no longer warm her body and the redness would disappear from her eyes. As she sat outside, surrounded by the children, a shadow darkened her world. Her body went icy cold. She knew it was the medicine man. As a child she had adored him. He would smile with pleasure at her playfulness. As she got older the adoration had turned into flirtation. She knew that she had affected him and she enjoyed the power she felt over the village spiritual healer.

When she was in her sixteenth year, it had happened. She had seen him from across the village and made her way casually to his dwelling. Her heart had beaten hard at the prospect of his touch. His eyes had traveled to her. He struggled to control his desire for he knew she would give herself to him if he wanted. The relationship would be frowned upon. He was many years her senior, and as her mother had made no marital connection between the two of them; he knew she would never be his.

Strong-Feather had seen him looking at her. She knew he had read her wanting thoughts. She waited for him to give her some sign. When he didn't, she disappeared behind the skin door of his dwelling. Waiting, she wondered why he didn't come. Time turned her desire into disappointment. Eventually, she realized that he was refuting her. Slowly, her feelings turned to anger. When she emerged from the dwelling, he was nowhere to be seen. She knew he had left the village. Alone, she vowed she would seek revenge for the unrequited love that now possessed her.

* * *

Courtney awoke an hour later with an unsettled feeling. She lay still wondering if Jack would come the following evening. The clock radio on the floor read that it was almost seven-thirty. If she hurried, she would make it to the mall before it closed at nine o'clock. She quickly made a sandwich to take with her.

The mall wasn't as busy as she had anticipated. A sexy lingerie shop caught her eye. Although the thought that Jack would even be remotely interested in picking up where they had left off seemed crazy, she stopped in the shop anyway. "Can I help you with anything?" A beautiful young salesgirl had snuck up behind Courtney. "Oh, you scared me half to death!" The young woman had an infectious laugh. "I'm sorry. Is there anything in particular you're looking for?" The woman smiled sweetly. "Sure. Do you have anything to win back the heart of a very special man?" The woman squinted and then drew her lips into a temporary tight circle. "Left things bad did you?" Courtney felt like crying. "Very. I slapped him." The salesgirl looked at Courtney in surprise. "Woops! Well, as you left it that bad, let's make you a good girl!" Courtney liked the young woman's style. She found out her name was Lucy. Lucy showed her a very sexy white teddy that opened down the front with several tiny pearl buttons. The bottom of the teddy unfastened. "Oh, my!" Courtney laughed. "Well, it's one of those things that he won't think you intentionally wore in the event things work out. You wouldn't want him thinking that you planned all this. You know men. It's all about control! A man hates to feel manipulated."

"You know what always works for me when my boyfriend and I fight?" Courtney gave Lucy a questioning look. "Catch them totally off guard right from the start! As soon as he walks in the door, do something special for him! Give him a gift. It doesn't have to be expensive, but it has to be personal." Lucy looked questioningly at Courtney. "Do you love him?" Courtney hesitated for a moment. "Yes. Yes, I do." The salesgirl smiled knowingly. "Ah, then what's the hesitation? You can't choke on those words when you tell him. Now, go get him that gift and practice the magic words, but don't over practice them to the point they sound insincere!" Courtney liked the salesgirl and thanked her for the advice. "I hope it all works out." As Courtney paid for the teddy, Lucy added, "Hey! Let me know how it all goes!"

Lucy had bolstered Courtney's spirit as she continued to search for the perfect gift for Jack. She stopped in a bookstore and searched until she found one of those cute little poetic books on the Art of

THE RED MASK

Forgiveness. Wanting to get him something more, she found the only jewelry store in the mall. She saw a simple gold tie clip. As the salesman approached, she told him she needed an inscription put on the clip. She asked if she could get the inscription done right away? "Well, you're in luck. Our jeweler just happens to be in this evening. What would you like inscribed?" He handed her a piece of paper and pen. Courtney wrote the inscription. 'J. I Love You. C.' The salesman looked at the paper. "If you come back in half and hour, it should be ready." Courtney put in the time by visiting the perfume counters in the large department store. She smelled and tested several scents until she found the soft scent that she wanted. She then went to the bedding section and purchased a feather duvet for the bed.

After picking up the tie clip, Courtney was already having second thoughts about the intimacy of the purchases. She imagined it wouldn't take Jack long to figure out he was being manipulated. She went home and waited anxiously for the next day to arrive.

* * *

Courtney spent Saturday morning cleaning the apartment from top to bottom. As a child, she had played a game in her mind. The prince was coming to take her away, but he wouldn't take her if her room was a mess. The game had originated from a recurring dream she had. She had always tried to keep her room neat in the event that the prince arrived.

She tried to rest on Saturday afternoon, but she kept going over the words she wanted to say to Jack. As they hadn't agreed on a time, she didn't know if she should make dinner, so she put together a fruit and cheese tray in the event that he arrived early. Around five o'clock, Courtney stepped into the shower and washed her hair. When she was finished, she gently removed the lace teddy from the tissue wrapping and thought about what Lucy had said. It shouldn't be an obvious attempt at seduction. She knew that if things got to that point, Jack would be able to put two-and-two together. The under wire section of the teddy pushed up her breasts making her laugh. "Who knew?" she said looking in the mirror. The tight bodice sucked at her waist making it look tiny. She loved the effect. Courtney pinned back her black silky hair, leaving wisps of hair hanging down her back and onto her shoulders. She applied the soft perfume to her neck, and between her now pushed up breasts.

"I Love You, Jack." She practiced the words over and over in the bathroom mirror. The words were indeed starting to lack sincerity so she stopped. As she reached for her mascara, she thought she saw a flash of red in the bathroom mirror. Her heart beat fervently in her chest. She assured herself that she had imagined it! "What do you want?" she asked as she looked into the mirror. "Why don't you just tell me and stop these games?" Her reflection stared back at her.

Six o'clock turned into seven, and Courtney was wishing she had set a firm time with Jack. He was torturing her by making her wait. It was shortly after eight o'clock when the buzzer sounded. Courtney's heart was now racing. She ran and buzzed the front door and then ran to the bathroom for one more look at her appearance. Courtney jumped in shock at the image that appeared in the mirror. This time, there was no denying the mask. It stared hauntingly back at her. Courtney jumped back against the wall behind her. She screamed in fear. She ran to the front door of the apartment and as she pulled the front door open, she saw him! "Well, hello Courtney. Looks like you've seen a ghost, or ... were you expecting someone else?" Courtney was speechless for a moment. "Yes, I was as a matter of fact! What the hell are you doing here?" Brad pushed open the door almost knocking Courtney over. "Get out, Brad!" Courtney went quickly for the door, but Brad was too quick. He put a hand out and slammed it shut. "I'm not going anywhere until we have a little talk!" Courtney's body was shaking in fear. "Brad, I've said all that I'm going to say to you. Now, get out of my apartment!" Brad Laduke spoke through clenched teeth. "Or what? I'm not leaving until we come to some sort of financial arrangement for what you owe me!" Courtney laughed nervously. "Oh, you must be kidding! I'm not giving you one red nickel!" Brad laughed an evil laugh. "Well, then maybe you can pay me back in some other way?" This was the last thing Courtney expected from Brad. "I wouldn't do that if I was you. I'm expecting my friend. I believe you two have met!"

The two small wrapped gifts on the kitchen table caught Brad's eye. "Oh, and what do we have here?" Before Courtney could get to the gifts, Brad had snatched them off of the table. "Give them to me Brad!" Brad quickly ripped the wrapping paper off of the small book.

THE RED MASK

"The Art of Forgiveness. How touching. Had a falling out, did you?" Courtney was seething with anger over Brad's intrusion into her personal life. "That's none of your damn business." Brad was already opening up the tie clip. "Oh, this looks valuable." Brad read the inscription. "Oh, isn't that so damn sweet! Well, it's of no value to me." Brad threw the tiny tie clip across the room. "I guess that just leaves one thing doesn't it?" Courtney started to back away towards the kitchen door. The intercom buzzed. The noise seemed to startle Brad just long enough for Courtney to run and push the speak button. "Help Me Jack!" Brad grabbed Courtney and gave her a hard push. She knew her shirt was ripped. She fell back hard, hitting her head against the handle of the fridge door. She fell heavily to the floor. Brad ran from the apartment.

Jack and Joe arrived to find Courtney lying on the kitchen floor in her apartment. "Oh God!" Jack yelled, as he quickly knelt beside Courtney. Joe yelled nervously at Jack. "Do you want me to call the police?" Jack yelled nervously back. "Joe, I am the police!" Under different circumstances, Courtney thought the exchange would have been funny. A small smile crept across her face. Joe responded. "Right!" Jack smiled down into Courtney's face catching the humor in the exchange. "I thought it was you. I just buzzed him in!" Tears fell from her eyes. Jack looked over at Joe. "Courtney has a nasty ex-boyfriend!" Joe nodded in agreement. Jack saw the torn wrapping paper on the floor. "Joe, can you get her a drink of water?" Jack picked up the small book entitled 'The Art of Forgiveness'. He knew it was intended for him. "Joe, stay with her. I'll be right back." Jack ran to the apartment staircase. He descended the stairs two at a time until he reached the parking lot. There was no sign of Brad. Jack proceeded to the street and looked in the cars that lined it, but there was nothing. "I'm not done with you!" he yelled. Jack returned to the apartment. Joe was still kneeling beside Courtney. Courtney and Joe both looked relieved when he returned.

Jack carried Courtney and laid her on the bed. He walked Joe to the door after a few minutes. "I'll stay here tonight, Joe. You don't have to worry." Joe was shaking his head. "What kind of man does this to such a nice girl?" Jack nodded agreement. "The wrong kind, Joe." As Joe left still shaking his head, Jack became riddled with guilt. If only he hadn't hesitated about coming. None of this would have happened. As he walked into the living room, he stepped on something small. He bent and picked up the small gold tie clip. As he read the inscription, his heart seemed to stop for a moment. He had been such a fool. Returning to the bedroom, he saw that Courtney appeared to be asleep. He had a difficult time rousing her. "Courtney. I think we'd better get you to a hospital." He noticed Courtney's torn shirt and unbuttoned the remainder of the buttons. "Oh dear God!" He was looking down at the very sexy lace teddy that she was wearing. Her soft breasts were beckoning him. "Come on Courtney. Sit up. He quickly went to her closet and grabbed another shirt. "Come on honey, we have to change your shirt." Courtney managed to oblige Jack, but her mind was totally out of focus. After changing Courtney's shirt, Jack checked her purse for health information and apartment keys. "Come on, darling." He picked Courtney up into his arms and carried her to his car. He drove quickly to the hospital emergency department. Looking over at her, he noticed that she was, once again, asleep.

* * *

The triage nurse was taking all of the necessary information from Jack. "Relationship?" she asked. Jack disliked the woman immediately for her sharp tone. He unfolded his hands that had been tightly entwined in his lap. "Spouse," he lied anxiously. "You can have a seat in the waiting room, Mr. Myers. Dr. Hanley will be with you shortly." Jack argued that he would like to be with his wife. The cool demeanor of the nurse was unaffected by Jack's demand. "Wait in the waiting room. You'll be called." Jack left frustrated by the curt command.

Jack paced back and forth across the waiting room floor for nearly an hour. He was just about to return to the emergency room desk when the doctor arrived. "Mr. Myers?" The older white-smocked man was looking directly at Jack. Jack anxiously extended a hand. "Jack," he said as a means of introduction. Dr. Hanley reciprocated the handshake and introduced himself. The older man led Jack to the seclusion of an empty examining room. "Your wife has a nasty head injury. She's still unconscious. We have completed a scan and have found a contusion on the back of her brain. Do you

THE RED MASK

know if your wife has suffered a previous head injury?"

Jack said he had no recollection of a previous head injury. The gray-haired doctor continued in a serious tone. "Well, obviously she's not going anywhere quick. We're doing our best to bring her around." Jack felt frustrated. "What is it? Is she in a coma?" Dr. Hanley didn't answer immediately. "Yes. With a grade three concussion, unconsciousness is often common. How did she hit her head?"

Jack should have been prepared for the question, but wasn't. "She fell." He hesitated again. "In the kitchen." Jack began to worry that the doctor would suspect that he had something to do with it. "I was out at the time. A friend and I found her." Jack thought that mentioning that he wasn't alone would alleviate any suspicion the doctor may have had. "Who was your friend?" Obviously, Dr. Hanley was suspicious. "I was with our superintendent." Jack had chosen the word 'our' carefully.

"Look, Dr. Hanley. I'm a police officer. I love this woman very much. I would never hurt her." The older man smiled his first smile. "No. I don't think you would. I just need to ask these questions. I think I'm a pretty good judge of character." Jack said he understood, but inside was thinking *'Not that good, doc.'* "Can I see her?" Dr. Hanley agreed.

Jack was surprised when he looked up at the black and white sign that read 'Intensive Care Unit (ICU)'. Dr. Hanley led him past the stop sign on the dual swinging doors that indicated that visitors must call by using the phone mounted on the wall beside the doors. Several bright orange doors dotted the long corridor that led to the nursing station. Before reaching the desk, Dr. Hanley turned and entered the last door. The room was where Courtney was.

The number of machines that she was hooked up to shook Jack. "Jesus!" He went to the side of the bed and took Courtney's hand gently in his. Her other hand had an intravenous tube taped to it. Dr. Hanley read the chart hanging at the base of the bed. Jack looked up to gage the doctor's reaction. "No change," Dr. Hanley said matter-of-factly. "So what does that mean?" Jack asked. "It means just that Jack. These things can last an hour, a day, or who knows?" Jack replied that it was the 'who knows' that he was concerned about. Dr. Hanley told Jack that a nurse would be in shortly. Before leaving the room, Dr. Hanley turned back towards Jack. "Talk to her. It may help."

Feeling alone in the room, Jack looked at Courtney. She was so beautiful lying there. "Courtney," he began. "I'm so sorry. I should have been there for you." Jack ran a hand through his hair. "I've been a real idiot. I do love you, so much."

A nurse entered the room, invading Jack's thoughts. Jack looked hopefully up at her as she added more information to the chart. The nurse was about to leave the room when Jack interrupted her departure. "Were you going to tell me anything?" The nurse exhaled. "I'll tell you something … when there is something to tell." She left the room abruptly.

Jack looked back at Courtney. "They're a real friendly bunch here darling. Maybe you could wake up so we can get the hell out of here!" Courtney didn't respond. "Oh, I see. Testing my love are you?" Jack chuckled. The sound of his laughter resonated around the hollow room.

Chapter 7

Jack awoke to a bustle of activity in the room. "Wake up, Mr. Myers. Your wife is awake." A nurse was gently shaking Jack, so as not to startle him. Jack felt a sharp pain descend from his neck down his spine. He had slept all night in the uncomfortable vinyl-clad chair. His attention turned to Courtney.

Jack reached over and held her hand. She looked at him and smiled. "Jack." Her eyes started to close again. "No, Courtney! Don't you close your eyes? Look at me!" Courtney was desperately trying to open her eyes, but the darkness was enveloping her, once again. She heard the distant "Wake up."

"She's gone again," one nurse chimed. "Oh no you don't," Jack commanded. "Come back here, Courtney." Courtney could hear Jack's distant beckoning. She struggled through the darkness towards the voice. She knew it was familiar. "Courtney, I need you to come back." Caught between the worlds of awake and asleep, Courtney saw the image of the medicine man before her. He was angry, and yet behind his anger, she was aware of a different emotion. "Don't leave me!" he said. "I need you here with me."

Courtney's eyes fluttered and then opened. She saw the familiar face in front of her. It was his. She continued to struggle to focus. *I know his name is Jack, but who is he?* "Stay here with me," he spoke softly. "Courtney, you're in the hospital. We need you to stay with us." Courtney didn't recognize the female voice that she now heard. Raising her hand to the back of her head, she saw the intravenous tube. "My head hurts," she gasped. The woman's voice continued. "Yes. You hit it pretty hard."

A stranger appeared in front of her. "Hello, Courtney. I'm Doctor

Hanley. You had us all quite worried." Dr. Hanley was studying the chart that the nurse had handed him. Courtney could feel the darkness enveloping her. "I'm here with your husband, Jack." Dr. Hanley shone a light into Courtney's eyes. Courtney tried to shake her head. "I'm not married." Dr. Hanley was shaking his head.

Courtney could sense that the stranger was uncomfortable. *We're not married,* she thought. Jack was looking at Dr. Hanley. "Don't worry. It won't last long. I've seen this type of thing before. It's just temporary." Dr. Hanley spoke soft instruction to the nurse, before leaving.

* * *

Jack had decided he had better call Courtney's parents to tell them about her condition. He found their telephone number through information, and hesitantly dialed their number. He felt a slight relief when after several rings, the answering machine kicked in. He hesitated before leaving a message for them to call him on his cell phone. He could only imagine their reaction when they received the call.

Courtney saw him when he entered. She was staring down at the tray of clear broth and jello that had been brought to her. He was laughing. "Looks yummy!" he said. Courtney was now looking at the tray in distaste. "I don't remember, Jack." He told her not to worry. "The doctor said it is just temporary. It'll all come back to you. Don't worry." Frowning, Courtney said, "What if it doesn't? I mean how can I remember your name is Jack, but not remember that you're my husband. When were we married? Where were we married? Do we have children?" There was clear panic evident in Courtney's voice.

Jack hesitated for a moment. "Courtney. We don't have any children." Courtney looked relieved. "I mean it's one thing to forget you're married, but to forget you have children …". Courtney's voice trailed off, as her eyes filled with tears.

"Courtney. We're not married!" Courtney turned her tear-streaked face towards Jack. "What are you talking about?" Jack looked nervously at the floor. "I just told them that in Emergency, so I could be with you." Courtney was looking at Jack with a blank expression. "Okay, so who are you then?" Jack was relieved that Courtney

THE RED MASK

wasn't calling for help at this point. He simply responded that he was a friend.

"I found you in your apartment. Your ex-fiancé did this to you. His name is Brad." Courtney reiterated the name and then shook her head. "I don't know any Brad." Jack smiled at Courtney. "Well, maybe that's not a bad thing. He's not a very nice guy." Courtney closed her eyes for a moment trying desperately to remember. She reached back and felt the pulsation in the back of her head. "What did he do to me?" Jack said he didn't know. "I think you must have hit your head. I found you on the floor in the kitchen. I'm guessing he pushed you."

Courtney was still looking confused, when a nurse entered the room. "Mrs. Myers. We're going to move you to a regular room. Dr. Hanley will be by later on to see how you are doing?" The nurse turned her attention to Jack. "Here's a plastic bag for her clothes, Mr. Myers. Someone will be down in a few minutes to move your wife." Jack looked at Courtney for her reaction. Courtney was looking at him with one raised eyebrow. Her reaction was curious.

After the nurse left the room, Jack smiled. "You missed your chance to rat me out." Courtney said she knew she had. "Maybe having a husband will come in handy." Jack asked how she figured that. "Well, maybe they'll send me home sooner, if they think there's someone to take care of me."

It was as Jack was gathering her clothes from the small closet in the room, that something triggered her first memory. *You'll want him to think it was his decision that things worked out. You know men.* The tiny buttons on the lace teddy had triggered the memory. Her mind drifted to the lingerie shop where she had purchased the teddy. Had she had a falling out with Jack or with this Brad guy? Courtney decided not to say anything.

* * *

The horizontal fluorescent lights on the stark white hospital ceiling were blinding. Courtney closed here eyes as her mind continued to struggle to make sense of her situation. After settling in her new room, Courtney was relieved when Dr. Hanley arrived. "Well hello there, Courtney. How nice of you to join us. How are you feeling?" Courtney responded that she was feeling fine except for the throbbing in the back of her head. "Any memories yet?" Something was familiar about the way his bifocals dangled on the end of his nose. "Actually, it's more like déjà vu. I feel like I've been here before. The way you're looking at me reminds me of someone." Courtney thought hard about the familiarity. "It's your glasses. My dad wears his like that. He's a doctor, too!"

Dr. Hanley looked over at Jack who was standing by the door to the room. Jack nodded. Both men smiled. "Tell me about your father, Courtney?" Courtney couldn't elaborate further. Dr. Hanley looked back at Jack. "Do her parents know about her condition?" Jack told him that he had left a message for them. "It would be good if she saw them. It may trigger some more memories." Jack agreed and said he would keep on trying them. "What's your maiden name, Courtney? Your father's name?" Jack answered before Courtney could think about the question. "Her maiden name is Myers. My name is O'Brien … Jack O'Brien." Dr. Hanley looked speculatively at Jack. "I see."

"Well, Courtney. I'd like to see you again, tomorrow. I think you'll remember a little bit more by then." Before leaving the room, Dr. Hanley asked Jack if he could see him outside for a moment. "Sure," Jack said hesitantly. Courtney had a feeling that Dr. Hanley had figured out that they weren't married.

Once outside of the room, Dr. Hanley looked Jack directly in the eyes. "Okay. Who are you?" Jack shoved his hands in the pockets of his jeans and shifted nervously. He was under scrutiny and didn't like the feeling. "It's very dangerous what you're doing?" Jack looked at the doctor. "She knows we're not married. I said I was her husband because I was dealing with nurse Ratched in your emergency department." Dr. Hanley looked down seemingly thinking. "Jack … we never had this conversation." With that, the older man turned on one heel and walked away from Jack. Jack saw him turn at the end of the corridor and could hear his fading footsteps.

* * *

Jack responded to the obvious distress on Courtney's face. "He thinks you're too beautiful to be married to me." Courtney smiled.

THE RED MASK

"Jack, what did he really say?" Jack took her hand in his. "He figured out the truth. Anyway, he's willing to let it drop. As far as perception, we're husband and wife." Courtney smiled sweetly. Jack couldn't help but think about how beautiful she was. *I Love Her.* He thought about how none of this should have happened to her. He wished Brad was in front of him right now. He would certainly be unable to control his hatred for the man.

"Courtney, do you remember anything about Brad?" Courtney shook her head. "We were engaged?" she asked. "Apparently ... at one time." Jack continued. "You told me he called it off just before your wedding." Courtney was desperately trying to remember. "Jack, why do you think I was engaged to such a jerk?" Jack didn't know how to answer the question. "Honestly, I don't know. Maybe you just didn't know him as well as you thought you did?"

Courtney asked Jack how they had met. "I found you asleep in your car with all of your belongings." Courtney figured she must have been running away from her failed relationship. Courtney appeared suddenly perplexed. "Jack, who's RYH?" Courtney was surprised that the acronym flashed so vividly in her mind. It dawned on him that Courtney was referring to the Royal York Hotel. Courtney could picture Robert Small and the department that she worked in. "See, it's coming back slowly. I told you it would." They were both pleased that she could remember a bit about where she worked.

Courtney closed her eyes trying to focus more intently on the vague memories she now possessed. *Call me Robert.* "Jack, I'm remembering him ... Robert Small. He is very nice." Jack was excited for her. "I'll call him in the morning for you." Courtney became concerned about not reporting for work. "Well, if he's as nice as you say, he should understand." Courtney had a feeling that he probably would understand.

"Courtney, I have something I need to do tonight. Do you think it would be okay if I came back in the morning?" Although she was reluctant to have him leave, she hid her concern. There was a growing familiarity about him. Something in his smile and the lines that stretched down his face triggered feelings within her. "Certainly. Yes. You've been great Jack. I'm sorry about all this." Jack told her not to worry. "We'll get through this honey." Courtney liked the endearment. Jack bent and kissed her gently on the forehead. She watched as the heavy hospital door slowly closed. He was gone. Her eyes closed. She couldn't help but wonder where he was going?

Chapter 8

The only sounds in the room came from the machines that surrounded Courtney. She sat alone, trying desperately to remember the past. In particular, she struggled with how Jack fit into the picture. She felt unsettled. She felt lost.

Sitting silently, she slowly thought back to the tiny buttons on the teddy that she had seen Jack pack for her. She wondered if it had been meant for him. She wished he were with her to fill in the blanks in her memory. The breath left her body, suddenly. She recounted an image of her hand slapping his face. Fear transcended her state of mind. She wondered instantly if he was actually her assailant and not this man named 'Brad' of whom she had no recollection.

She continued to try and remember why she could so vividly see the scratch she had left on his face. There was a feeling of being confined ... trapped, but that was as much as her mind would allow her to see. A mistrust of him slowly built inside of her. "Oh, my God," she whispered. Courtney thought about how he would be returning the next day, and how he had convinced everyone that he was her husband ... except ... Dr. Hanley!

I need to speak with him, she thought. *I need to tell Dr. Hanley my fears!* She immediately paged the floor nurse and a few seconds later the nurse appeared in Courtney's room. Courtney asked her if she could speak to Dr. Hanley. "He's not in tonight, Mrs. Myers. I'm sure he'll be by in the morning. Is there something you need?" Not wishing to complicate things with the nurse, Courtney said it could wait. "Do you know what time he makes his rounds?" The nurse said she thought early. "I'll leave a note for him to see you first, if you like?" Courtney thanked her.

* * *

Strong-Feather stood frozen in front of the medicine man. He had always had this strange ability to read her, and she knew that he was aware of her plan to escape the village that night.

She had told no one of the return of her vision. It had happened so gradually. At first, it had only been an ability to see shadowy images. Now, she could see as clearly as before. She had kept up the façade of blindness. If they thought she couldn't see, then they would be less likely to suspect her plan of escape.

As he looked into her eyes, she wondered if he could tell. He looked suddenly past her. His face had changed. Strong-Feather turned to see what had caught his attention. There was nothing. As she turned back to look at him, she saw the smile on his face. He had tricked her into revealing the new reality of her vision. Her body trembled.

Looking around to see if they were being watched, he took her hand softly in his. He led her to the dwelling where he had taken away her vision. He hadn't expected that her sight would return as quickly as it had. He had hoped that the traveler would be gone by the time it returned. Strong-Feather feared that this time he would take it away forever. She now accepted her fate.

Her vision didn't matter in the darkness. She could hear the rhythm of his breath. As she stood in fear, she felt his hands softly touch her face. She wasn't sure why he touched her in such a gentle way. The backs of his hands ran down her neck to the gentle curves of her breasts. They continued to her tiny waist and she felt a release of emotion, realizing that he wasn't going to hurt her. His strong arms wrapped around her back and pulled her longingly into his body. Her fear turned to the deep desire she had once felt.

He told her she must leave. She told him she couldn't. She knew she felt a desire for him that she would never feel with the traveler. He hated the traveler, but he feared the outcome if she stayed. He had wanted to run with her, but there was nowhere safe for them. They would be found. They would be killed. She yelled her protestation. He put a hand over her mouth to silence her. Removing his hand, he replaced it with the desire of his lips on her hers. She responded instantly.

THE RED MASK

His hands wrapped through the silky darkness of her hair. As the kiss deepened, he laid her where he had before. This time, he lay beside her running one hand up the softness of her thigh. Her body ached with the love she felt for him. She begged him to take her away. She felt him tense with the deep desire of his passion to have her with him always. He told her she must remember him. As the love between them intensified and they united in the love they felt, Strong-Feather vowed that she would never forget. The culmination of their love would provide her with a lasting proof. There was no child in her womb until that day. No one would ever know the truth. No one would know, except Courtney.

Courtney awoke with a start. The familiar sounds of the hospital equipment beat rhythmically in the hospital room. The dream remained fresh in her mind. The child had been that of the medicine man. She reentered the fog of her dreams. This time her dream was of Jack O'Brien.

* * *

Jack pulled his car in front of the Laduke home and sat alone in the darkness. His drive to Midland had been one of tremendous thought and apprehension. He hated this man for what he had done to Courtney. He viewed him as a coward. He longed for the chance to confront him man-to-man.

The Buick sat parked in the driveway. Jack had figured that it was probably unlikely that the sedan belonged to Brad. Jack continued to wait for over an hour in the darkness of his car. He was just contemplating going to talk to Brad's parents when the lights of the pick-up came up behind where he was parked. The truck turned and parked behind the Park Avenue.

As Brad exited the truck, he was shocked to see the larger man standing in front of him. "What do you want?" he asked angrily. "I'd like to see what kind of man assaults a woman and then runs like a scared rabbit." Brad said he had no idea what Jack was talking about. "Why don't you try a little harder, pal?"

Jack could sense Brad's fear. "Just like I thought," Jack began. "You're not so tough now are you?" Brad struggled with his words. "Get ... get out of here!" Jack laughed. "Or what? I'm not here to listen to your crap. I'm here to tell you if you ever come near her again, I'll beat you senseless. Do we understand one another?" Brad stood silent. "Sorry. I didn't hear you." Brad nodded, looking down at the ground. "Damn right you'd better agree." Jack turned and walked back to his car. As he drove away, he could see Brad. He was still standing leaning against his truck. His head was hung.

* * *

Courtney's dreams had returned to Strong-Feather. She could feel the deep true love that her ancestral grandmother had felt. Their love had been gentle yet filled with deep emotion. She felt the inevitable demise of the relationship and the sickness that consumed Strong-Feather. How could she leave him now, knowing they were destined to be one?

The fates had conspired against them. He was smart enough to know that if she stayed, not only would the Huron village not approve of the relationship; they both would be eventually killed by the Iroquois. He was the medicine man. He was the healer of the village. He could not leave, despite the love he felt for the beautiful young woman. All he could do was save her. All he could give her was one night, one brief testament of his love for her.

She had begged him to allow her to stay. He had told her she could not. Things were worse now with the Iroquois. She had pleaded with him to run with her. Again, he told her he must stay. "You will die. They will kill you." He knew his fate. "I will join you, where the sky meets the heaven. We will be together. I promise you. Go with him. You must for the sake of our love." She knew. She knew she would have more to protect. The warmth of his love had created a gift. She knew it, intuitively. "I will wait for you, where the sky meets the heaven," she had said. "I will meet you there, my love."

Strong-Feather would leave with the traveler that night. She hid the love she had felt in her heart. She had already died inside. She couldn't have predicted that she would join him soon. She would die giving birth to the child. The child would carry the legacy of their unfulfilled earthly love.

* * *

THE RED MASK

Courtney awoke at six-fifteen, anxious to see Dr. Hanley. An hour later, the room door opened and a younger doctor appeared. "Hello Courtney. Dr. Hanley asked me to look in on you. How are you feeling today?" Courtney said her memory was still blurry. "Where's ... where's Dr. Hanley?" The young man told her that unfortunately Dr. Hanley's mother had taken ill. "I'm afraid he had to leave town for a few days." Courtney was thrown by the news. The doctor noted her agitation.

"You are already making progress. It's just a matter of time. You will have to trust me." Courtney wanted to trust the man in the soft green hospital uniform. She wanted to share her suspicion. "I'm in all day. I'll check back in with you in a little while." Courtney thanked the doctor before he started towards the door to the room. Courtney watched as the soft green slippers that covered his shoes, disappeared behind the door.

The second hand on the clock ticked time slowly away. The long Black Hand would move backward before it moved forward. The soft ticking sound lulled her back into a state of unconsciousness.

The door opened just after ten o'clock, and Jack appeared behind a beautiful floral arrangement. Although smiling gratefully, Courtney was actually dealing internally with her feeling of mistrust. "Good morning, beautiful." Courtney knew she must look a sight and she let Jack know that. "Oh, I don't know," he added smugly. "There's something very sexy about you right now. You're looking particularly vulnerable in that blue hospital gown with that I.V. strapped to your hand. Of course, I've seen what's beneath the gown, so maybe it's just my imagination taking over." Courtney was at a loss for words. "Well, maybe you have. However, as I don't remember the occasion, your comment doesn't mean anything to me." There was sharpness in her tone that caught Jack off guard. "Yes. I did assume you would remember. I've obviously offended you. I apologize."

"Was Dr. Hanley by today?" Courtney reluctantly told Jack about Dr. Hanley's mother. Jack appeared concerned. "I called your boss today. He's quite worried about you. He told me to tell you not to worry." Jack smiled. "He even said he would cover your desk, as long as you promise to come back. I told him I'd keep him informed of your condition." Courtney thanked Jack. The clock continued to tick slowly. Both Courtney and Jack looked up at it in unison. Thankfully, a nurse entered the room, breaking the uncomfortable silence.

"Good news, Mrs. Myers. We can take that I.V. out. Now that you're on solid food, you won't be needing that." Courtney was thankful that the needle would be removed from her hand. A bruise was present where they had struggled to put the needle in. Courtney gingerly rubbed the bruised area after the nurse removed the I.V. Jack took her hand and looked sympathetically at the bruise. *He's very good at hiding what he's truly about*, she thought. *Maybe it's guilt for having put me here in the first place.*

After the nurse left, Courtney told Jack that he didn't have to stay. "Don't be silly, honey." The endearment made her shudder. "I took today off to be with you." Courtney asked him what he did. "I'm a police officer." Fear traveled through her body. Her mind told her she shouldn't trust cops.

To make matters worse, the young doctor returned to the room. Jack stood and introduced himself to the doctor. The doctor extended a hand to Jack. Courtney focused on the way the two hands joined. "Michael," he said. "Michael Mann." The young doctor turned his attention on Courtney. "Good news, Mrs. Myers. Your husband can take you home today." The sentence was hard for Courtney to digest. "I spoke to Dr. Hanley and we agree that seeing familiar surroundings may trigger some more memories for you." Dr. Mann was smiling expectantly as Courtney. He couldn't have predicted the fear in her eyes. Courtney exploded. "Well that's just plain crazy. I can't leave here!" The young doctor responded gently. "Now, now. This is a good thing. You'll be with your husband." Courtney began. "He's ... he's not ...". The doctor responded quickly. "No. Dr. Hanley won't be back for at least a week. He said you're in good hands." Dr. Mann removed a business card from his pocket. "I'll want you to call my office, if there's any news. Set up an appointment with my office for Friday. I'll want to see you then. Oh, and no driving." Courtney was thinking that she could be dead by Friday. "Dr. Mann, can't I just stay here?" The doctor reiterated Dr. Hanley's instruction. "Really, Mrs. Myers. He thinks it's for the best." Courtney looked over at Jack. He was sitting back in the hospital room visitor chair. His arms were folded across his chest. There was a look of deep concern on his face.

THE RED MASK

* * *

Courtney rode in silence beside Jack. The small car made her feel claustrophobic. She could sense when he looked over at her, and she recoiled deeper within herself. Courtney desperately wanted to be back at the apartment, so she could escape him.

As Jack parked the car, she was surprised when he turned off the ignition. He grabbed the paper bag that housed her few personal items and got out of the car. Opening her door, she said, "Jack, this isn't necessary. I'm okay now." Jack let out a low laugh. "What are you talking about? You've been released in my care. You can't remember anything. I'm coming up. Besides, do you even remember your apartment number?" Courtney shot back the answer. "Two hundred and twelve! There were two hundred and twelve of them!" Jack looked puzzled. "What are you talking about?" Courtney was confused. She told him she wasn't sure. "Apparently, you're confused about something." Courtney could see the bones. She shook her head to remove the picture from her mind. "Okay. Come up. But, I don't need you to stay." Jack was silent.

As Courtney opened the door to her apartment, she had a sudden flashback. She felt her body being thrown backwards, and the sharp pain intensified in the back of her head. She had a strange feeling that she had felt the pain before. She saw the older man in front of her. "Are you okay ... uh, miss?" Courtney instinctively nodded that she was. Jack re-entered her world. "Courtney? What's up?" Courtney looked over at him. "I'm not sure. I'm confused." Jack started towards her, but Courtney put up her right hand. "I ... I don't know what's going on here." Jack asked her if she thought he had done this to her. Courtney didn't answer. "I'm tired, I guess." Courtney went to her bedroom. Jack could hear the bed being moved in front of the bedroom door. "Jesus!" he exclaimed.

* * *

Jack walked softly to the bedroom door. "Courtney," he offered gently. "Come on, Courtney. Talk to me, please?" Courtney met his pleas with silence. "I know you're afraid. I guess I would be too. I would never hurt you, honey." Courtney still didn't respond. Jack's voice was distant and she liked it that way. "Look Courtney. Joe was with me. He knows I didn't do this to you. If you won't talk to me, would you at least talk to him?"

Courtney sat for a moment confused. The name 'Joe' was familiar to her. "Who's Joe?" she yelled through the door. "He's the superintendent. We found you ... together." Courtney was struggling trying to put a face to the name. "Look Courtney. Let me in. I have something to show you." Courtney struggled with the decision to move the bed, but she knew she couldn't stay in the bedroom forever. "Fine!" she said defiantly.

After moving the bed, the bedroom door opened. Courtney's eyes readjusted to the light of the hallway. "What is it?" Jack reached in his pocket and pulled out the engraved tie clip. As she read the inscription, Courtney felt a rush of emotion. The object was familiar. Obviously she had felt enough love for him at one time as to display it on a gift. *Maybe I was wrong? Maybe I just thought I loved him?*

The deep look of concern on Jack's face was intensifying her confusion. *How could such a concerned look not be genuine?* She wanted to cry out and ask God for the answer. "Alright. Let me speak to this ... Joe!"

Jack left and returned back with Joe. The little man shyly entered the bedroom. "We've been so worried. " He took one of Courtney's hands in his. Courtney apologized for not remembering him, although there was a nagging familiarity about him. "It's okay. You must have hit your head pretty good. You were unconscious." Courtney asked Joe if he knew her ex-boyfriend. "No. No, I don't know him. You don't remember?" Courtney told the small man that she didn't remember Brad. "I think him no nice."

Courtney looked back at Jack. She could see the concern on his face. There was no denying he was a handsome man. She wanted to trust him. Courtney hated that she couldn't. Something just wasn't right. Joe interrupted her thoughts. "My wife, Maria. I tell her everything. She hopes you better soon. She prays for you." Courtney knew that Maria was familiar to her. "Yes. Please tell her I need to see her." The little man smiled. "Sure. Sure. She likes to see you, too. She good person, too." Before leaving, Joe squeezed her hand. "Yes. I tell her."

After Joe left, Courtney stood looking blankly at Jack. She

THE RED MASK

wished he would leave. He elicited disarray in her world. Jack's words confused her. "Courtney. I wish you would get better. I don't understand. I feel so connected to you. It's like we were meant to be together." Courtney told him she was tired. Jack reluctantly left the room.

* * *

As Courtney lay in her new bed, she found she was thinking of Jack on the uncomfortable gaudy looking couch in her living room. She was tempted to go and see if he was awake. She struggled with any details of her relationship with him. Scattered images played with her mind. An image of another face entered her mind. The face was filled with anger and maliciousness. She surmised it had to be Brad. A flood of memory came to her. He was holding the tiny book in his hand. The book was entitled 'The Art of Forgiveness'. The entire scene played out in her mind. She saw him toss the tiny tie clip across the room. She remembered the buzz of the intercom and her plea for Jack's help. Courtney sat and wondered if her memories were intact, or if she had just created them.

Another image flashed through her mind. She was standing outside of the village beside the pole where the mask was hanging. Darkness enveloped her. Her eyes were wet with sadness. The traveler came. He smiled gently at her. She knew she didn't love him. She loved another. The traveler was unaware of her feelings for the medicine man. He felt the moistness on her face and assumed that her sadness was caused because she must leave the village. "Mon Cherie," he whispered. "Je t'aime." She knew he loved her. She must hide her feelings to protect what grew inside of her. They disappeared into the shadows of the night. The medicine man stood and watched. He vowed that he would find her. He vowed that they would be together for all time. He walked softly over to the red mask. Removing it from its perch, he held it up to his face. He was unaware that the village was surrounded. The Iroquois had arrived. He would not live to see the morning light.

Chapter 9

The light of the hospital room assaulted Courtney's senses. She struggled to make sense of her surroundings. Although it looked somewhat familiar, the room had changed. It was smaller than she remembered. She looked towards the chair that Jack had sat in. The vinyl-clad chair was not there. A blue and white striped curtain hung on the left side of the bed. She wondered where she was.

A nurse appeared from the other side of the curtain. The nurse seemed as surprised as Courtney was. "Miss Myers!" she exclaimed. "Welcome back! I'll ... I'll get the doctor!" The nurse disappeared. *Why am I here?* Courtney had remembered being in the hospital. *Why is this room different?* She wondered what had happened to bring her back to the hospital.

The room door opened and Jack appeared. Courtney felt relief at the sight of him. Jack was looking at her strangely. "Miss Myers? How are you feeling?" Courtney smiled at him. "Good ... Jack." He seemed puzzled. Courtney was confused for a second. "Cut it out! You're Jack ... Jack O'Brien." The handsome man smiled. "Yes. I'm Jack O'Brien. Dr. Jack O'Brien. But, how do you know that?" Courtney looked at the doctors' clothes on Jack. "I ... I don't understand. You're Jack." Jack O'Brien stood before her. He looked over at the hospital nurse. "We need to call her parents." The nurse nodded and left the room.

"Miss Myers. You're in Huronia Hospital in Midland." Courtney wondered why she was there. "You had a car accident. I'm afraid you hit your head pretty hard." Courtney was totally confused by the information that Jack was giving her. "I don't understand Jack. Brad did this." Jack O'Brien looked at her sympathetically. "No. You hit your head in your car. You were at Discovery Harbor." Discovery Harbor was 'her place'. Her mind traveled back to the accident. She had told the older man that she was okay. "No. You're wrong. You're Jack. I met you in Toronto. You're a police officer." The young doctor continued his sympathetic look. "No. This is the first time we've formally met. I'm an intern here. Your father is a doctor here at the hospital. I work with him."

Courtney yelled, "Stop it. You're Jack O'Brien. You found me the apartment. I'm in love with you. Why are you doing this?" The young man seemed concerned. "Look. Your father will be here soon. He will help you remember. I'm sorry." Courtney wondered if it was all a dream. She knew Jack. She loved Jack. Why was he pretending to be a stranger to her? The hospital door swung open. Her father came rushing over to the hospital bed.

"Dad!" she exclaimed. "Oh, honey. We've been so worried." Courtney looked at her father for explanation. "I don't understand, Dad!" Her father smiled softly at her. "I know. You've been in a coma for two weeks. We've been so worried. It's okay. We're so happy you've come back. Let me tell you what happened."

Courtney's father told her about the car accident. Courtney lay stunned by the information. He told her how Brad had ended the engagement. He told her about the accident at Discovery Harbor where Courtney had blacked out. "They brought you here. We've been so worried. It's been two weeks, honey." Courtney was in shock. "Dad, I know him." Courtney was pointing to Jack O'Brien. Dr. Myers smiled. "Jack is working with me. He's an intern here. He's helped tremendously. When your mother and I aren't here, he is. He's a good doctor Courtney. I'm proud to have him on board."

Jack O'Brien smiled at Courtney. Courtney saw the same familiar laugh lines. She knew him. She knew the gentle way he cared for her. She knew that he was kind. She knew that she was intended to be with him. "Come," she said softly to him. "Thank you. I'm still confused by all of this, but I know you are important to me." Jack smiled softly at her. "Courtney, I don't know all of the details. I'd like to help, if I can?" Courtney laughed. "Someone has told you that you should. Someone has told me that I must accept your help. I see … I see a red mask." Jack O'Brien stood confused. "Sometimes, I see a red mask in my dreams." Courtney smiled. "Then we need to talk. We need to find out why?"

Courtney's father interrupted the exchange. "Courtney, we have so much we need to figure out. But for now, realize that we were all worried about you and we're all glad you're back." Courtney smiled at her father. She had so many questions. She needed answers to help her deal with the situation. "Dad, who's Dr. Hanley?" Her father hesitated wondering how much information he should impart to his daughter. "He's a specialist I called in. He's from Toronto. We met a few years ago at a conference at the Royal York. He's a good doctor, Courtney. Unfortunately, he's been called away. His mother is quite ill."

The hospital room door swung open. Eve Myers appeared in front of her daughter. "Honey. Oh, thank God! Are you okay, darling?" Courtney smiled at her mother. "I think so. There is just so much. I'm trying to figure out so much, mom." Courtney's mother reached out and wrapped her arms around her daughter. "Oh honey. I'm so sorry. Brad was just awful to you. You didn't deserve this. We've taken care of everything. He wasn't the one. He just wasn't the one."

Courtney looked over at Jack O'Brien. "Somehow, I know that mom." Jack O'Brien smiled the smile that she had seen so often in her dreams. She had so many unanswered questions. There was so much she needed to know. "Mom, who is Michael Mann?" Her mother looked at her blankly. "I don't know, sweetheart. Why?" She told her mother of her dream of the doctor. "I'm sorry, honey. If it was Medicine Man, I could understand." Courtney sat blankly. *Medicine Man. Michael Mann. The Medicine Man was Jack.* It all seemed impossible. "Oh mom, there's so much I need to know. I need your help." Her mother smiled gently. "I'll help you darling. You know I'll help you." Courtney reached for her mother's hand. "You need to tell me about the red mask." Her mother's color changed. She was ghostly white.

Her father had interrupted the conversation. "Courtney. You can talk to your mother later about all that. We need to attend to your physical well-being first." Courtney's father noted her vitals and then shone a small light in both of her eyes. When he was finished, she blinked the vision of the light away. He stood above her. She could sense that he felt great relief as he looked at her. "You had us worried." Courtney said she hadn't meant to. Her father smiled a half smile. "No. I'm sure you didn't."

"Can someone please tell me what happened?" Although the question was directed at the group, it was her mother that she was looking at. She would, at least, provide some details. Her father would only give the abridged version of events. Eve Myers began.

"Well, we're not even clear why you were at the Harbor." Courtney's place was always a secret from her parents. She felt that everyone should have a place like that. A place where they could just sit, meditate and reflect. Her mother continued. "We found out after, that Brad called off the marriage. We called the Laduke's as soon as all of this happened. Do you remember that he called off the wedding?" Courtney smiled and nodded that she did. "Well, it was quite a shock to everyone. We're sorry, honey."

The memory of the night that Brad had called off the marriage seemed so long ago. So much had happened in Courtney's mind since that time. The young doctor stood as the Jack in her dreams had. His arms were folded across his chest. It was hard for Courtney to read his thoughts. The look of concern on his face seemed genuine. A glimmer of a smile appeared on his mouth. Courtney realized she was staring at him. She blushed slightly and focused on fondling the stiff hospital sheet that covered her from the waist down.

"Anyway," her mother broke the awkward silence. "We're not clear how the accident happened? The nice man who called for an ambulance said your car just veered over and then you overcorrected and went hard into the ditch." Courtney agreed. "Yes. I remember veering in front of him, but I didn't think it was a ditch. I know I hit the shoulder and then my head whipped back when I stopped. I remember he was very kind, mom." Her mother nodded agreement. "Yes. He's called several times to see how you are. His name is Robert Small." Courtney felt like she had landed in Oz. All of the characters in her dream were actual people. She wondered about Joe, Maria, Paula and Anita. The image of Anita entered her mind. It was Jodie. She remembered that Anita had reminded her of Jodie when they had lunch, but she had not visualized them as the same. It had been a feeling ... only a feeling. She knew she would make the connection with the other characters in her mind. It was going to take time to separate the dream from reality.

THE RED MASK

"You said I've been here two weeks?" Her father answered. "Two weeks, honey." Courtney was surprised that she had only been there for two weeks. "Dr. Hanley. Is his first name Joe?" Her father looked surprised by the question. "Why ... yes. Have I mentioned him before?" Courtney told her father she didn't remember. She struggled with the question she truly wanted to ask. She hesitated before turning to her mother. "Mom. They found an ossuary, didn't they?" Her mother was puzzled by the question. "Honey, I don't understand. How do you know about that?" Courtney told her of her dream of being in Little Lake Park. "It was eerie. Nothing was moving. I should have known something was wrong. I should have known." Her mother moved softly and held her hand. "How could you have known? I don't understand how you knew about it. They were digging at the new arena. They hit it by accident. There were over two hundred bodies." Courtney informed her mother that there were two hundred and twelve. The room was silent. Courtney knew instinctively that the ossuary was hit after she had her accident. "Hocus, pocus," her father added. Courtney laughed. "I knew you were going to say that dad!" Jack O'Brien chuckled.

As if reading her mind, he asked, "So Dorothy. How do I fit into this picture?" Courtney smiled. She looked at his hands. There was no wedding band there. She wanted to tell him about her dreams of him. She wanted to tell him everything. She looked at the curious looks on her parents' faces. Courtney simply smiled. She looked into the eyes of the stranger that she knew so well. He was her medicine man. The medicine man had brought him to her. He was her destiny. "I think we need to talk." Courtney laughed. "Alone." Jack O'Brien laughed the laugh she had heard so often. "Apparently."

*

Printed in the United States
34817LVS00002B/64-111